A coming of age story, Shades of Luz is refreshing to read because it is empty of dysfunctional types of characters. The novel is about a decent man who has realistic fears, desires, family and friends. Gorman is able to keep one's interest without having to incorporate the typical, often pointless, themes of violence and sex that many authors resort to in order to secure readership.
-Weam Namou - author of *The Feminine Art* and *The Mismatched Braid*

With a happy facility for words—and interesting, fresh choices of words at that—John Gorman shapes Shades of Luz into an antic, frantic, cockeyed search for love and meaning. Like every human being in his or our world, Benny has managed to get into jobs that baffle him, control him, evade him—and fallen in love with the marvelous Luz, who baffles him, controls him and evades him too. This wonderfully odd story introduces us to a marvelously inventive universe with tough guys, loony broads, jazz-playing monkeys and surprises that can change lives.
- Karen Heuler, author of "*The Soft Room*"

"A charming and original coming-of-age story. As if Hieronymus Bosch and Ralph Bakshi had a love child. Filled with sentences that reel and careen like a roller-coaster ride before they hit you with cartoon punches. You'll be knocked off-balance but eventually you'll be pulled back toward the center, where you'll find a love story with a very big heart."
-E. R. Catalano

Shades of Luz

John Gorman

ALL THINGS

THAT MATTER

PRESS

Shades of Luz
Copyright © 2009 by John Gorman

This is a work of fiction. Any resemblance to actual persons, living or dead, is purely coincidental.

ISBN: 978-0-9840984-7-7
ISBN: 0-9840984-7-X
Library of Congress Control Number: 2009908704

Cover design by All Things That Matter Press

Cover photo By: dani, HOUSE OF SIMS,
http://www.flickr.com/photos/houseofsims/3382635653/

Published in 2009 by All Things That Matter Press

Acknowledgments

Thanks to Karen Heuler, Wah-Ming Chang, Elizabeth Catalano, Margo Landau, Schuyler Bishop, and Tamara Anderson who have seen a metamorphosis take place with this book. Each of you shared tremendous feedback and commentary. I offer a special thanks and blessing to my parents who have always inspired the best in me. Mom and Dad I love you both. I dedicate this book to all the writing teachers I have ever had. Last, but not least, I offer a special dedication to Alejandra Cadena-Perez who provided me with an invaluable muse.

Seems Like Déjà Vu All Over Again

From where I sat, strapped in my metal leg-clamps, it stirred like Guernica. Patches of blue and gray swirled into a giant hologram beyond its plasma screen.

"Have a look-see Benny, at your brain," Mungo said, pointing his knobby finger at my head. "You've swallowed enough books."

The creepy image waggled like no brain I'd ever seen. There weren't just pages, footnotes, and prologues cached in there, but barcodes, thumbprints and doggy ears. My palms dripped cool clay-stinking sweat.

"You've got two choices," Mungo said, "Run away, but I guarantee we'll find you. Or face the music and pay your dues."

I've never taken ultimatums well. Then again, I've never really dealt with much conflict. The one thing I was sure of was that I wanted to see Luz again. She hadn't smashed through my protean shell at that point; she'd only teased her way into my life.

Luz, my precious boomerang, brought joy back into my life filling, me with substance, heartache, and maple-drenched pancakes when she couldn't polish off hers. She loved watching me struggle—with everything—contributing her winning smile, all cheeks and teeth, gnawing right through my inhibition and gunnysacking my nucleus. Nobody had ever penetrated my being, but she wasn't up for reciprocity. So long as I was content with the scraps she offered we would be fine, but I wasn't, craving bigger portions.

It all started back when I was twenty-eight, soon to be twenty-nine and still living with my parents while trying to tie the knot on my thesis. Quite frankly, I was hoping for a miracle. That one day I'd see the thesis had completed itself. Don't get me wrong I wasn't lazy, but sometimes my imagination stalled. Here I was capable of storing tomes in my head, and I kept bumbling over stale minutia. Filled with conflicting thoughts, I was easily distracted.

My thesis topic meant absolutely zilch to me. The whole while I kept picturing a room of faculty advisors shaking their heads, giving a synchronized thumbs down. As I left this room, the faculty advisors rubbed their palms together eager to shame the next sucker. Why support more professor wannabes? Anthropology journals were so damn esoteric, so specialized that maybe a dozen dorks in the world knew how to decipher the text.

Forget that. I wanted to write something useful, for humanity. Hell, I would've settled for original. Yet I worried somebody in Brussels, Rio or Katmandu was having the same idea and knew how to implement and execute a full-fledged game plan.

Prior to the bookstore incident, I hadn't the foggiest notion where I was going, professionally, personally or otherwise and it really bugged me everybody else seemed surefooted. Maybe my soul's compass snapped its needle.

Each day I feared getting trapped in the hallway by one of my neighbors who loved reminding me of how much I'd grown then mussed my hair. They spoke to me as though I was still a child, but in many ways, they weren't off the mark. Nobody to blame, but myself. My parents, God bless them, were the kind that hoped I'd stay with them forever. The sad part was I wouldn't have minded either, not really, except for the way people looked at me and what they must have thought. The local busybodies had a good laugh about it, how I couldn't get my act together, laying around all day watching the idiot box. There goes Benny, wasn't he the first kid on the block with the bright blue Big Wheels? Remember how smart he looked in his school uniform. What a good boy he is grocery shopping with his mom. Nobody had to say it, but I felt it deep inside me. Public opinion was, hands down, my sharpest thorn. It would hamstring me from reaching my potential.

So I might as well admit it, I was the product of a working class family determined to give their only son everything they never had. Dad hailed from Brooklyn and Mom came from the Lower East Side. Together they began a new life in Rego Park lusting for a fresh patch of green. Didn't matter to them the grass pushed through pavement cracks, the point was they'd done better than their parents and their parents' parents. Right across from the building I grew up there was, still is, a park. Back then we called it 'Dirt Park,' for good reason, because, aside from the steely tangle of Monkey Bars and the decrepit, splinter-inducing swings there was nothing but dirt. Mounds of it. Nobody knows for sure how many Match Box cars and Star Wars figures lay buried there, but now it's wall to wall green. You could putt off the lawn, if the old farts who guard their gated enclave would let you.

Way back, 'Dirt Park' was my training ground, a tired, homely field of dreams where I learned to bat my first balls. Dad lived to show off his pint-sized prodigy. He changed his shift and spent his days with me, then worked through the night, but the game never stopped there. We brought our exuberance home with us and took turns with a Whiffleball bat smashing rubber-band-wound socks from master to junior bedroom. Up to a point, Mom indulged, but once her dry wreathes or potpourri baskets got piñataed she drew the line, barging in on us, pointing her knitting needles – that's when we took our chill pill.

Dad pledged to make a ball player out of me and as a kid I had great promise. I really slugged the ball. I was never a home run hitter, but I tagged shots to any part of the field, bingled sliders over the shortstop's head. My on-base percentage soared into the slugging percentage stratosphere and my room was chockablock with trophies.

The trouble with me was I'd play one year then took off the next. I'd always pick up and drop things and though Dad hounded me to stick with it he never forced me and Mom didn't seem to mind. In fact, she thought it made me well-rounded, trying new things. I'm not blaming my parents, it wasn't their fault, but maybe, if I'd had the ruler-cracking brand that locked me in my room until the homework was done instead of doing it for me, then maybe I'd be a somebody instead of a knucklehead.

My day came and it frightened me. There was nowhere to hide from the wicked bolt of destiny that rocked me. I'm always getting way ahead of myself because all these nuggets keep pulsing in my head so, when I tell my life story a myriad of thoughts rattle me at once and sometimes I can only offer mediocre tangents. This time, I want to make clear how things got out of hand. How did I get so mixed up? Good question. Maybe I'm a magnet for problems. Maybe it has something to do with being an only child.

This photographic memory everybody's accused me of having can all be traced back to a childhood trauma when I saw Mom clipping my pictures from the family album. A numbing cast entombed my heart. Each careful snip, sheaths like micro follicles whisked to the ground. My head barely rose above Mom's waist so with a slight crouch I hid behind the table spying on her. Fresh sliced melon kissed the air, a plate perched on the table. I reached and knocked over Mom's blue and white-trimmed Ginori, shattering it to shards all on account of my fixation of being clipped from the album, clipped from the family.

To prevent this from happening I holed up in my room, absorbing every picky-uny detail. If I sponged my surroundings: photos, memories, objects I'd safeguard my spot in the family. Now, my thought process wasn't intricate and full of philosophical mumbo jumbo, but in my own way I had a Cartesian epiphany. Trouble was, in my mind, I became those pictures. I couldn't separate my own savory memories from the pictures.

The force of habit spilled into everything I did. Books weren't read but devoured. Each page, every detail, the appendix, everything, doodles in the margin, coffee, cocoa stains. Before long, my whale of a memory nailed down things I hadn't the faintest clue what I was gorging. Formulas filled my head. I sneezed and out came Fermat's Theorem.

Relief only came from scribbling it out of my head. Oftentimes it got so clogged purging the words seemed useless, which was why I drew pictures. That, too, came out like so much muck. My drawing was pitiful. My magnum opus achieved at the age of five, a watercolor of Shogun Warriors battling Minute Men, anachronistic to say the least but my sense of perspective, bullets in the background, bludgeoned swords in the foreground, showed the prowess of at least an eight-year-old. Still, art was not my calling.

I suppose that's the price for having such a ravenous memory. I couldn't, after all, have an omnivorous mind and Goya's brush.

Libraries and bookstores, as you might imagine, became my stomping grounds. I found great refuge slumping my head over a book. They were my friends, even the ones on accounting and cooking. It was as if they wanted to share their secrets with me. Hold up a conch shell and hear the ocean. When I held up a book and flipped through the pages, letting them flutter, I heard the authors' voices. Even closed they whispered to me, but when I'd read they morphed into beings, sometimes rising high like stain glass windows, other times they fit on my pinky, like a ladybug.

This was intimacy as I'd known it. I had a tapeworm, but instead of in my gut, it gerrymandered into my head. I wasn't dumped by my family, so I prayed to keep my photographic memory, believing it secured my place.

One day, minding my own business as I always had, I left the bookstore a bit earlier than usual because I needed to run some errands for Mom, who wasn't feeling too well. Tylenol topped the list, followed by shaving cream, cucumbers, ginger ale, beer nuts, and let's not forget the packaged chicken soup – because boiling water was my specialty. Chicken soup it was. That's what piddled through my head, chicken soup, the moment I set off the metal detector. Now, I had never triggered the bookstore's detector, occasionally the libraries' because if you brought a book from another branch this would inevitably happen.

The security guard with his crooked smirk escorted me through the store with all the busybodies gawking at me as the two of us marched past a handful of clerks trying to maintain order by the half price racks. He led me down a narrow corridor, down the stairs, into what I imagined to be a janitor's closet. "Mungo will see you now," the security guard said.

There, to my surprise I saw behind a huge desk with a neatly folded stack of papers, a husky man hunkered forward blowing green bubbles.

Beside him stood a neckless specimen who kept missing the bubbles with his hands.

The room reeked of cheap-grade Windex and mildew.

Across from the desk was a shiny red gumball machine. The husky man was Mungo. He dropped a penny into the machine. Cranked the handle and out spat half a dozen gumballs. He leaned to the side, positioning himself so as not to miss any, both his hands cupped under the metal spout. The elastic in his suspenders playfully, almost mockingly slung him back into an upright position while he crammed his mouth full of ammo.

Two goons dunked me into a chair, slapped on arm and leg bands so that I locked in place. Then they stuffed a wired helmet over my head. Down with a whump dropped a giant plasma screen.

"I swear I didn't take anything," I said. "This is all a big mistake."

"Welcome to my humble abode," Mungo said.

I squirmed so that my keys might fall out, the stupid gizmo keychain that I carried around, compass, whistle, all-in-one that was a surefire way to hold up the line at any airport since it looked a heck of lot like a box cutter.

"Let me show you the culprit," I said, tucking my lip between my teeth so as not to reveal any unwelcome trembling. "This keychain has done it before. So if you'll just let me demonstrate I'm sure we'll all be happier."

They laughed.

Mungo's hairline receded to the point where a yarmulke or a party hat would no longer be sufficient enough to mask his baldness. For somebody with such a large mouth he didn't take full advantage of his masticatory apparatus. He nibbled his gum as if trying to dislodge a bit of nut or some other petty food particle, then the stretchy green bulb sprouted from his lips. Sometimes he kept it there until it popped or deflated. It seemed part of him, a colorful goiter.

Lulu was his right hand thug garbed in a pineapple-patterned rayon shirt over stonewashed dungarees. He kept his arms propped in a muscle man pose. Frankly, he didn't look like he could stow his arms by his sides. He wasn't mega buff. He just didn't seem flexible. I bet a shiny nickel he spent too much time flexing in the mirror. Lulu then did the itsy bitsy spider in a tight range eight or so inches above his collarbone as if intent on disproving my thoughts.

"Don't be cutesy," Mungo said staring dead at me. Lulu swiveled clockwise.

"I'm not," I said. "I'm just a working stiff who likes to unwind by reading new books."

"Your story is touching," Mungo continued, "but we've brought you here for a serious matter. Got any idea what's going on upstairs?" he said pointing to my head.

"Think so."

"How about explaining yourself to Mile O' Books? You've ripped them off since you were a snot-nosed punk, before the big chains and all these faggy coffee shops."

"I don't get it."

"Oh, you don't. Then get a load of this."

Within seconds a hologram projected from the screen. The blue fluorescent glob swished while the outer region stayed gray. This was what made me think of Guernica, although Picasso's piece was done on a flat surface whereas this was more of a finger painting evolving into a creepy sculpture.

"Benny, this is your brain," Mungo said, pointing his knobby finger at my head.

The second glob grew bulkier, gyrating in unctuous coils and left me in a woozy state. The infrared scan dissolved the glob and out splattered thousands of words, barcodes and price tags. I shuddered, wondering if they'd strain this alphanumeric soup out of my brain.

"That's everything you gobbled up today alone," Mungo said tracing the image of my brain with a red laser pen.

"He's like a sponge," Lulu added, knitting his unibrow.

"I swear I didn't do anything."

"But Benny, it's all there on the screen. See for yourself. That's why you tripped the metal detector."

"It's a crazy misunderstanding."

"You calling me a fruitcake," Mungo said.

"Of course not."

"Your head is all whacked up, a book slut."

"How is this possible? How do you really know me?"

"Look, we don't want to bore you with the particulars. Finding what you want is a piece of cake nowadays. Thank you very much technology. Let's just say I also know about your little scavenging habit. Don't tell me you really need all those Glenn Campbell records, marzipan, and all that other bunk."

His knowing about my scavenging with fellow slacker Brig scared me the same way I peed in my pants in first grade but sat paralyzed in my desk.

"The truth is Benny you can't hide from you. This gift doesn't have to be your albatross. Stop being selfish and help us out."

"I'll do whatever you want. I'll sweep floors, wash the windows, but you can't put this on my record."

"You're a walking library, kid. I've got a string of special assignments and I could use a good head. Help isn't so easy to come by nowadays. How are you with numbers?"

"Lousy."

"Perfect. We don't need any smart ass know-it-alls. We need somebody ripe. Good fruit is hard to come by too with all this organic crap squishing out the juicy goodness we used to get in the old days. Ever been apple-picking?"

"No."

"Well, we're in that line, too. Got some of the best orchards in Warwick. I'm nuts about Cortlands. They aren't as chewy as Macintosh, and to tell you the truth, Red Delicious are beginning to taste like candle wax. Know what I mean?"

This fruit fetish seemed odd with his pouch crammed full of gum.

"We'll go over that another time. You won't be picking apples, I assure you."

Down came another screen with a multitude of lines and captioned titles connected to each other. "Video Pirates" and "Dart-slingers" struck my curiosity.

"You will be schooled in everything you need to know. Don't think we don't know about your little side business. We've made all the arrangements for you to keep your usual routine. You'll be weaned away from that before you know it. But we need to act fast otherwise we'll get a late start and I can't stand for any tardiness. Right, Lulu?"

Lulu, pinching his unibrow, nodded.

"Life's all about showing up, but that don't mean nothing unless you get there early. Got it?"

That was the assignment, showing up, and as usual when confronted with a problem I ran the other way. In this case however, one might consider mine an act of bravery since these thugs weren't exactly partnering with the girl scouts. Any defiance would surely have meant death or in the very least permanent mutilation. I took a gargantuan chance ducking from them and returned to my street-vending routine, but found a new post.

A Girl Named Luz, A Hippo Named Cyclopes

Two months earlier, I was peddling plush toys from a duffel bag. So help me, we went door to door. We haggled local merchants, dog-walkers, whoever was kind enough to lend an ear. I never had trouble emptying my bag, but there were many casualties, as we said in the biz. Most of the prospective peddlers went AWOL their first week, many the first day. You needed a certain je ne sais quois to lug around a bag of stuffed animals and get people to buy from you.

How in the world did I get hooked into the stuffed animal racket? Wish I could say there was a better explanation, other than the truth, which was I'd circled it in a newspaper ad, and, I might add, was duped. I'll get to that part later.

The advertisement offered the chance to make serious coin while helping poor kids in third world countries. This piqued my curiosity. When I'd gotten to the interview there were many shmoes like myself all there for the very same reason, desperate to work. Meanwhile, the interviewer assumed that the six other interviewees, and myself, were engrossed by his slide presentation. We were ready to leap into action and end global poverty and plunk down a first payment on a brand new Audi.

By nature, I'm a healthy skeptic with a daub of naivety. Just as well because if you look at this urban jungle too long you only see cracks in the pavement and miss out on the little joys like the smell of hot pretzels, being able to prop your feet on an empty subway seat, air vents blowing up skirts, the well-placed billboard mustache.

Halfway through the slide presentation,four skedaddled. Now maybe I was more desperate than the others, more gullible. It's a shrink's wet dream to analyze my perceived enthusiasm, but I was there, ready and willing to help my fellow man, so long as it involved a paycheck. The rest of the altruism fit into my breast pocket. Competition was fierce. There were the purse, belt, golf-shirt and gaudy tie vendors, not to mention the kitsch photographers and curbside masseuses.

Our job was much more nomadic than the other street vendors, much more akin to leafletters and ladies of the night. Not that I was an expert regarding the latter, but I've, once or twice, followed a streetwalker, just to ask a question or two. Nomads have always fascinated me, but I'll be honest the first few times I tailed a hooker were a bit scary. Imagine if I got nabbed by an undercover cop. So far I've never been booked [get the little pun] but I worry that my excuse, playing the curious urban anthropologist, might not always pan out. A chatty hooker makes the time fly by; some of them however, can be rather pushy if you're not there strictly for business.

They schooled me in the art of bilking money. The lucky apprentices and myself grabbed our bags from the dispatcher in Greenpoint then lugged it over to Midtown, where, since I was a greenhorn, a mentor shadowed my every move till I was confident enough to shake people down for whatever they would throw us, usually just to get us out of their faces. By noon, I was the only sucker left.

Chalked it up as an experience and for the record my resume was pitiful, filled with mime jobs in department stores spritzing new fragrances and various pet and plant-sitting gigs. You can take the prick out of a cactus but you can't take the cactus out of the prick.

My forte was acquiring dead end jobs hardly a notch above what just off-the-boat immigrants would do for a buck or Ivy Leaguers slumming for a summer until they anchored themselves into their six-figure niche.

Ipso facto I dove into the stuffed animal business. This is when I met Luz, though I was certain I'd seen her before. I was up to my armpits in koalas and down to my last hippo, which some kid had plucked the eye out of, don't ask me how, so nobody wanted it. Luz had this enchanted expression as if I were peddling the remains of a lost civilization instead of stuffed animals. I busied myself pretending I didn't see her, my heart pounding Morse code double-time expanding my aura.

Nobody leveled me with such an undertow of ethereal charm. Everything scrambled inside me when she pulled near. She examined my merchandise of teddies, turtles, and then bent over to pick up an orange octopus. Then she began to toy with its fuzzy tentacles. She stood up joggling her purse strap back onto her shoulder to get a more holistic view of my goods.

"You don't have any pandas," she said, petting the octopus's nose.

"No, actually we don't, but we have a heck of lot of koalas as you can see."

"No monkeys either."

"Fresh out. If you were here three minutes ago, you could've had yourself a marmoset. I'll put one aside for you when I get the next batch."

"That's okay. I mean, I wouldn't want to put you to any trouble."

"None at all. That's my job."

"Hiding stuffed animals from potential customers."

"Making people happy."

"It really isn't for me. It's for my niece."

"All the same."

She discovered the tag on the octopus's bottom and proceeded to scrunch her brows. The folds on her forehead like little ripples in a pond. She nodded to herself then held the tag out.

"So is this true? The money goes to the children in Somalia?"

"I'm sorry about that," I said, biting off the tag.

Then crumpled it up and tossed it into the sewer behind the curb.

"So you're a crook."

"No, not at all I swear I just found out about that the other day. I've gone completely solo, I don't even work for that organization anymore."

"It would be a travesty."

"I'm well aware, but hey, please have it. Your niece shouldn't have to suffer from the slings and arrows of outrageous hoopla."

"No, she shouldn't."

"She'll love it, a gift from me to her."

"She's not supposed to take gifts from strangers."

"Well then, you're the ombudsman. You're not a stranger, you're her aunt. Technically, she's going to take the octopus from you so that's okay, all you really have do is accept it from me. I'm sure you can handle that. Call it my jab at goodwill."

She hugged it close to her chest.

"I couldn't. How much is it?"

"Either that one or Cyclops the hippo."

"What happened to him?"

"It's a rough business finding these orphans a proper home. I think I have an eye patch somewhere."

It was a while before she returned. Nonetheless, as promised, I'd kept a marmoset aside for her, casting off many pushy people desperate for stuffed monkeys. Call me a closet romantic, but I was sure she'd be back. After all, I'd felt the ground tilt below my feet when we met.

When she returned she refused the monkey, opting for a green panther. It was this second time that we had what I'd like to consider more meaningful banter, though I still knew hardly anything about her except for her name, her affinity for stuffed animals and that she had three dozen pairs of flip flops. I'd managed to find out she was planning on doing a documentary on Luddites. I nodded, more so in acknowledgement that such old-fashioned thinking could survive in this day and age, though I did find her topic fascinating. There was a brief moment, in which I got the feeling she was sorry she had mentioned anything. Then it occurred to me that perhaps, she had broken the sacred anthropological tenet not to inform a potential informant. I didn't take it so badly it just never dawned on me somebody might see me as the kind of guy who'd thumb his nose at progress.

I was somewhat hesitant about broaching the subject of my half-baked thesis with her, but somehow she squeaked it out of me. She also had an interesting suggestion to motivate my progress.

"Don't get me wrong you have a certain knack for stuffed animals," Luz said, "But I can see you selling books?"

"Books?" I repeated.

"Well, how many interesting conversations can you scrounge up pawning off pandas?"

"I met you."

"That's true, but couldn't you turn your table into something more productive. Maybe you can study the buying habits of your customers. Wouldn't that be an interesting slant for your thesis? Actually, I guess you could do a comparison. Sell stuffed animals, books, bootleg videos. Mix it up."

"You might just have something there. That would probably make the most sense, applying my job to my thesis, but the thing is I have a certain reason for doing my topic."

"Oh."

"Maybe it's a bit stupid for me to fix on this topic now since I have been bouncing around for way too long, but I'm trying to find out something about myself. See, I pick up and drop things so much that I never really build a suitable layer of integrity. Call me nuts, but I feel that the thesis I work on needs to be on a topic I have absolutely no interest in, but if I can somehow tie the knot on it, it just might give me the boost I need."

"Sounds like you've put a lot of thought into this."

"Your idea is great and I probably would love to do it, but the way I am I probably would change my mind halfway through and pick up a new topic. I'm a mess."

"No, I don't think it's that, but you need to have a little more confidence in yourself. I think you're going to do big things someday. This documentary I'm working on could be a bit tedious so you're probably better off doing your own thing."

I felt really crappy about opening myself up to her. She rattled my sense of stasis. I so enjoyed talking with her. I wanted to be a part of something, anything with her. I would have actually paid her to be a part of the documentary, but I couldn't keep from stuffing my foot in my mouth. I was infatuated with the arc of her smile and the way she tilted her chin listening to me. As far as I was concerned, it was only the two of us there even though crowds of people hurried this way and that, taxis whizzed by. Once in a while, I shed a glance at the passing city. My eyes needed a break because I had a tendency to stare too hard. I didn't want her to think I was a freak.

Still, to her credit, I decided to dump the animals and sell used books. My mobile bookstand would become my sanctuary, after I locked horns with Mungo. After I'd met the big guy I wouldn't set foot into another one of those book behemoths, God forbid I set off another detector.

While I was building my mobile bookstand I met Brig. He was on a quest to discover the enlightened chess opening. That's what willed him over to my table. Had I met him a few days earlier Brig would have seen me peddling stuffed buffalo instead of books. I made the major faux pas telling him I'd leafed through some of Pandofini's chess books. He laughed thinking that I'd made a joke.

"He's a chess chump," Brig said, collating dandruff from hair to hand as if he were at some point about to roll dice. "I'll be back tomorrow same time."

"Look, I'll do what I can but I'm not promising anything."

"One lousy book, is that too much to ask?" Brig said, squatting on all fours just to make sure I wasn't clowning him by keeping the good stash underneath the table.

Nothing could sway him. He associated me with chess because I made that stupid comment about chesswonk Pandolfini the first time he crossed my path, so he kept bugging me about chess books. Baby ducks fall into this same trap, following anything that moves during their critical imprinting stage. I'm not a mother figure though and Brig isn't a duck, but he does waddle the way he walks. I'm still not convinced that Homo Sapiens have evolved past ducks because we slug through our lives in a continuous imprinting mode. After all, isn't that why we put so much effort into making first impressions?

Brig didn't meet me peddling plush pandas though, he met me selling books, so, for whatever reason, I humored him. He introduced me to the scavenging scene and whenever we did our rounds, we'd stop for a while and play a few games. He didn't care if I sucked he just wanted to see me make the effort.

In some warped way, I'm glad he dripped into my life.

We tore through garage sales, college hallways. Books poked their ears out of the most unusual places, including Laundromats. I gobbled them whole and he spat out anything unrelated to chess. We dug through garbage. It became our religion and we weren't alone. It became trendy after a while which meant that there was less coconut cream pies, blenders, vintage Glenn Campbell, Sex Pistols and Engelbert Humperdinck albums to go around.

We didn't do it because we were bums, but because we were tired of waste and, quite frankly, you could find all kinds of goodies in there like video game consoles and untrammeled boxes of Oreos. We didn't go for the health food shit the way some of the other scavengers did, we were pirates, in a way, off to discover booty. When I spotted something really spectacular it was childhood Christmas revisited.

For me this was a thrill, not so much to fill the grit and grunge of some primal need, whereas you couldn't tell with Brig the way he licked the crumbs off his Fu Manchu after an urban excavation.

Chessnut Delivers Fortune Cookie Message

I waited months for Luz to come back to see what I had done, to thank her for pushing me into this new direction. She'd have no choice but to let me buy her a cup of coffee.

One day while I was packing up early she snuck up on me and begged me for the marmoset, again when I was out of them. She left with a polka dotted giraffe and a long face. There was something on her mind, but I didn't graft it. She crossed the street and a huge bus, one of those Hamptons Jitneys blotted her out. I craned my head a few times, but I couldn't make heads or tails which way she'd gone. Poof, she disappeared, as if she was never there.

That cute little way she pet stuffed animals as though they were real kept shoehorning its way into my daily routines teasing me, o ye of flim flickering faith. What else was there to do but bury myself in books? So easily I lost myself while selling them, reading them or pontificating about them. That was my triple threat.

Brig was always around and even when I picked a different spot he somehow found me. It was a bit disturbing, but I sympathized with him and his cockeyed quest to become a chess grandmaster. I wasn't sure what he used to do. He was a bit evasive whenever I probed, but it seemed to me he had once had a decent job doing something or another probably with numbers.

He wrapped his legs tilting his head, yogi in training, brooding over his position trying to telepathically lure his army across the board, only the wind was too strong or his balsam cut pieces too frail to stand their ground.

We had an agreement worked out that whenever I couldn't find him his chess books, which he diligently lobbied for, that I would squat across from him and spar until he knocked the stuffing out of me.

He usually found good digs for me, many classics, the occasional first and second editions and enough *National Geographics* for me to start my own curbside dentist's office. I hardly reciprocated. Still, he visited me, with his toothy grin and sagging mustache often having the uncanny knack for sneaking up on me just when I was in the midst of dumping off a significant batch of books, to a paying customer.

He ambushed me as I was reaching for the money. Lumped himself onto the edge of the table so that it naturally tipped over, but he still held onto this most unusual specimen. My customer got that squeamish look as though we might jump him.

Brig flashed his Chucky Cheese grin holding up what sort of resembled a phallic-looking Buddha, not the blimpy ones you see perched on some crunchy's mantelpiece, this was a gaunt thing, Buddha hit Slimfast, gone cold turkey on boneless spare ribs, pork fried rice, French fries, Yodels, chili dogs, beer-battered onion rings. Brig must've seen this circumcised Buddha as a bishop the way he fondled its blunt scalp.

My customer had left, not that caterpillar mouth seemed to care, but an apologetic nod would've been nice.

"With all the kids on break you can't just pick up a game in the park?" I said.

"What's eating you?" Brig said, stuffing his little prize into his pocket.

"Nothing, I'm just a bit edgy, but that doesn't mean I want you poking your nose around here every two seconds. There are lots of pilgrims you can spar with."

"Don't flatter yourself. You're a stinking pawn pusher."

"And is there a problem with that?" I said dusting off some merchandise.

"Not if you can live with it. But I have this hunch that's not enough. Am I right?"

"Look, I'm just a street stiff who loves to read, the way you love to play chess. We're just gnawing through two different cobs of corn."

"Hmm, so that's the problem."

"I wouldn't quite call it a problem. It's just the way it is."

"And just like that you're content."

"Maybe you would call it complacent. I've come to terms with the way my life is and live it as such. I don't have anything against a little game here and there, but it doesn't consume me the way it does some of those galoots in the park who'll hustle you out of your lunch money."

"Let me tell you something, chess is life."

"For me it's not."

"For everybody. You just don't realize it."

"It's just a poor substitute for reifying Medieval Times on a plank of cardboard."

"Don't get on such a high horse. Things haven't changed so much. You can chalk up all the medical and technological advances to post-Darwinian sorcery. We still live by the swing of a sword. Dragons, Kings, vassals."

"I disagree with what you say but I'll defend to –"

"That's flattering. This is strictly business. Don't think I've got all the time in the world to hook you in today, not when I'm just starting to get a handle on the subtle nuances of the Ruy Lopez. Some pokes just can't get it through their thick skulls that every sacrifice isn't a tried and true gambit, not that I'd even liken the Ruy Lopez to one, just so you know where I'm coming from, but you know that part where you can bag the king's pawn if your rook is covering the E file, well, that's where I was having a bit of trouble, if you must know. You wouldn't believe me if I told you I've got this amazing novelty on the twenty-third variation so let me just say I'm not going to tango with you today. Just a word of advice, do what Mungo tells you to do."

"What?"

"Forget about playing stupid. I know everything. That's precisely why the big hump sent me over. He figured you'd try to weasel your way out. Eyes are everywhere. Let's just say you haven't a clue what he knows and can still dig up on you. Don't try fighting it. There's no way out now. Just submit. With a bit of luck you'll only come out with a few scratches."

"What if others are peeking into my head?"

"Don't be so curious. The less petty shit you worry about the better off you'll be. Sometimes ignorance is bliss."

Reporting For Duty

The arrangements had already been made even before I went back to the bookstore to ask Mungo where, when, and how I would start. Lulu gave me a crayon-scrawled badge and I brought it with me to the Plex, a drab building in midtown with windows that needed a good hard scrub. The guards nodded as I passed the greeter's desk as though I'd been working there for years. They didn't even look at my badge.

Up to the thirty-ninth floor I went. My stomach swished like sea monkeys ready to pop into phase two. When I got off the elevator, I saw the receptionist poking at her teeth with a toothpick. She had a compact in her other hand. When she noticed me spying on her she snapped the compact shut. The light on her headset bleeped and she began speaking to the caller.

I grabbed the less lumpier seat in the waiting area, angled it away from the receptionist. I left my backpack slung over my shoulders. It gave me a certain blanky level of comfort. My stomach wouldn't stop gurgling and I regretted not picking up my usual, street vendor coffee and a Boston cream. A well-worn copy of *Sporting News* caught my eye and I perused it to ease myself into my new employment setting. The thought of Mungo's thugs bumrushing me still had me loopy. I licked my thumb to turn the page over and check out the National League's box scores, when the receptionist, still donning her headset, snuck up on me.

"You look just like my cousin Nelson," she said. "Hi, I'm Doty. Gal Friday five days a week."

"Benny," I said shaking hands. Boy, hers were clammier than mackerel.

"First days always suck," Doty said.

My stomach gurgled in agreement.

"How about a cup of Joe and maybe a snack?"

I followed her down the hall. Her flip flops whapped the soles of her feet with the sound of a precocious bullwhip. She wore Japanese farmer pants with the drawstring untied and untucked. I sweated in my Glenn Plaid suit, my backpack now cradled in the crook of my left arm. I felt my roll-on deodorant dripping down my pits.

The kitchen looked like the inside of a Winnebago, a misshapen stack of fruit baskets lined the back wall. The fridge's busted handle sat on the counter next to two brown-stained paper bags.

"You like jelly donuts," Doty asked.

"Love'm," I lied.

I hated the sticky sugary goop that glommed onto my fingers. She poured two cups of coffee. I waved her off when she offered non dairy creamer and hoped she would leave me alone so I could spit out the yuck in my mouth. She flashed me a toothy grin. Her left incisor was partially chipped and kind of jaundiced. I got the distinct, wacky feeling she wanted to wipe the sugar off my mouth. I stopped eating and cursed her cousin Nelson to myself.

After the snack, she led me to the cubicle where I was supposed to sit and read over a binder. Not a peep from me. I didn't so much as want to clear my throat and draw her attention. Every so often she checked up on me. The minute she turned and left I continued solitaire tic tac toe. How many times was I going to stare at charts with squiggly lines? I imagined constellations, spiral galaxies, heart palpitations. I was a reader not a mathematician. Mungo asked me if I was good with numbers and I told him flat out no. Why did I have to toil over something I sucked at?

A few minutes to four, I was called into a room where two doofy guys debated the information I internalized that day. Their wild gesticulations cast batty shadows over the part of the screen that showed the numerous charts and frames I devoured. After a bit, I realized that I'd been racking my head full of stock trading patterns.

"How did you come up with this?" the instructor rebuked, pointer prominent at my nose as I dipped back ready to parry.

"Just soaked it up," I replied.

"Hmm, so you saw the base at the left of the two hundred day moving pattern."

"That Little Dipper thingamabob," I said.

"That's what you saw?"

"That's what I was supposed to see?"

He loped over to the other instructor and they traded meaningful nods. Spat out short monosyllabic gibberish. The bottom line for me was another crash course, this time schooled in the shapes and patterns of pork bellies and currency, the spitting images of stock movements. Some came in flying saucers, flexing biceps; there were many fundamental shapes to become acquainted. Once I was given the green light, I had my first chance to cram in a room full of other grunts.

We had to chant, "The richer we'll make Mungo." By day two, the nub of a room was filled with a dozen grunts. Elbow to elbow we took notes with the efficiency of Sanskrit stenographers. We'd all been recruited to work in the Plex, but I was hand-picked by Mungo himself.

One piss, one coffee break a day and lunch was a dash to the hotdog stand. On the spot, any of us were forced to rattle off what we had memorized. Our instructors moped about with their clipboards and jotted down their jottings. It soon became known that I was Mungo's fair-haired boy and then the other grunts fazed me out of their sightscape. All but one, Charlie who filled me on the inside dope. I'd become part of an ad hoc information-gathering cohort consisting of hackers, grifters, onetime money mavens fallen from grace, and a few saps, like myself, who hadn't the balls to run out of this upscale sweatshop.

Charlie, the self-absorbed pantywaist, told me in confidence that most of us wouldn't cut the mustard. He muzzled his sneezes into girlie achoos which I suspected might be signals to the higher ups peeking through nano-sized cameras. Maybe I was too neurotic, but Charlie kept wiggling his glassy eyes around the room even into the waste basket littered with thousands of jagged paper slivers, a hand-torn shred-job I thought. When I asked him if he was alright he admitted to being hopped up on meds, Amoxicillin Tri-k. Yum, one of my ne plus ultra favorites. Lulling there like a raw yucca stick, he knifed his shoulders tight so as not to reveal his oblong sweat stains underneath his armpits. The sporadic growth of pimples on his chin underlined with razor nicks.

He plowed right into his chirpy diatribes about the Plex. Who the past flavors of the month had been, grunts with promise that petered out, and the few lucky ones. I got the impression he wanted to gas my head with negative crud because he was shitting a brick thinking I was there to take his place.

People have always found me as a barnacle to barge onto, runny-nosed smurfs swinging nets at me rather than butterflies, toothless bag ladies plump with deposit cans, eager to show me their cheesecake. Somebody once told me I had an approachable face. So I let it grow grizzly. Did it keep them away from me? Hell no, they came out in full force. Freaks with an unquenchable thirst for split pea soup and the breath to prove it lined up for directions or to sell me their patent anal hair remover. Would you mind very much taking my picture mooning that hotdog vendor? This was an everyday occurrence for your friendly neighborhood Sisyphus trying to dodge the biggest boulders, but they kept bounding onto me. This was part of the reason I left my portable bookstand and here I was clumped into a corporate shoebox with Charlie sneezing in my ear.

He cupped his coffee two-handed, sometimes trading it back and forth as a hot potato.

"I hear napkins and handles enrich the drinking experience," I said.

"They never stock milk around here. This powdered shit tastes like kitty litter," Charlie said.

"Know what you mean."

Charlie looked at my giant Styrofoam cup with lusty eyes.

"Gimme some of your coffee," Charlie said clumsily reaching for it.
"I'd rather not."

"What you think I've got cooties?"

"You're sick."

"Suit yourself, but let me give you a piece of advice. If the big boys waltz in here you kiss their pinkie rings."

"Roger, Charlie," I said holding a mock salute under my brow.

He tore through the sugar packets and sculpted a white mountain onto his palm before licking off the peak. The leftovers, he drizzled into his puny paper cup. Another grunt poked his head into the kitchen for two seconds and left after a muffled message wheezed out of the speakers. Charlie tilted his head and began digging gunk out of his ear.

"When did you know you were a freak?" he asked me.

"We had to memorize the Bill of Rights back in fourth grade. The brightest kids were too slow. It took them half the week before they had the first five down pat. I knocked off the first ten in fifteen minutes, including the Preamble."

"What did your teacher think?"

"She thought I'd had a jump start since I was the type of kid who always read ahead. She busted my chops. My teachers had the impression I was a sniffling showoff. While the other kids were stuck on 'Curious George,' I was up to 'Encyclopedia Brown' and when they got to 'Gulliver's Travels,' I was reading Wittgenstein. I wasn't a showoff, it just came easy and I loved sharing what I knew. The trouble with me was I never knew when to shut up. When I knew I had this freakish gift I bottled it in, but my teachers still thought, and understandably so, I was reading ahead."

"You didn't want the other kids thinking you were a weirdo so you bit the bullet?"

"Naturally, I became a bit of a wise ass to cover my tracks."

"I hated raising my hand. I'd get all antsy about answering in front of girls. I goofed the simplest answers."

"If I could do it over again I would've stuck to my guns. I always give in too easy."

Perhaps this is not the best foot to get off on, but I wasn't there to impress Charlie.

"Was there just a toot toot?" Charlie said curling his bottom lip.

"From the speakers?"

"Yeah, like five minutes ago."

"No way. We have to scat."

He left his mess on the table and together we zipped into the hall. The first door on the left had a bigger room than we were relegated to, but the grunts there had binders twice the size of ours and had to underline their entries in fat florescent markers.

"No, thanks," Charlie said. "It may suck now but we're moving to bigger and better things."

"Where are we off to?" I said as we passed a gutted corridor, sheetrock aplenty propped against the left wall. Enough dust to clog a rhino's sinuses.

The average grunt's lifespan was five months, which made sense to me. Charlie was a veteran of eighteen months, by far the most senior in logged hours and age. Thirty-twoish I told him. He took the Fifth, his prerogative my loss.

Ahem, Dartboard Theory, Is It?

We were greeted by a fellow in a grubby lab coat. His name was Gus and he chaperoned the dart-slinging monkey room. Two humans, but only one monkey, were allowed in the room at any given time. This was strictly followed so as to prevent too much mammalian mimicry. The object was to keep things as random as possible. The monkeys were kept in holding cells, but they had a beautifully painted mural of St. Tropez or Lagos.

Gus coached through the Plexiglas. On the outside of the door two numbered ladders hung by copper thumbtacks, one ranked the monkeys and the other ranked the trainers. The term trainer was really a misnomer, but who was I, at that point, to make a stink.

Newspaper clippings lined the walls. Rudy, last year's crackerjack, watched over his monkey, Nietzsche. Rudy's name topped the ladder outside. He had good rapport with Nietzsche, the lone Rhesus of the lot. Nietzsche made three quick dart tosses each a foot apart from each ticker symbol. Rudy waited behind the masking tape on the floor, the line of demarcation where a monkey needed to stand in order to make his toss. Nietzsche gave his trainer a high-five.

Nobody knew what boomers would boom at least for a week although short-swing breakouts happened by market close. Boomer, referred to a stock that was going to bust through its resistance level and soar into a new stratosphere. No guarantees, but this was the accepted premise. There was no tickertape of any kind in the room. According to Gus, the monkeys might grow smitten with the flashing glow of certain ticker symbols and thus skew the random element driving dart board theory. It occurred to me that even if the monkeys were drawn to a glowing symbol that didn't mean they weren't going to tag that respective stock. Stereoscopic vision or not, the monkeys didn't see such blurry newsprint from their vantage point.

A note on random. It was widely accepted that any stock could bolt into its own orbit, plunge into disrepute, or mosey ad nauseum sideways without a care in the world. The point being, that no cocksure dweeb could cook enough data to prove that his theories rocked the pure and accidental.

"Charlie, you and the new guy are up," Gus said.

We waited by the door until Rudy came out with Nietzsche. Gus pulled Nietzsche by his fury digits and led him to his holding cell.

"Should we wait," I said.

"Nah, let's warm up," Charlie said.

"What do you mean?"

"We're getting fresh monkeys," Charlie said, "Maybe even a couple that have never tossed a dart before. We'll need to break them in."

No sooner did Charlie finish cracking his knuckles did Gus return with two new monkeys. One was a snow monkey the other was a macaque. Charlie tossed a couple of darts, neither of which stuck to the wall. His monkey almost seemed to be laughing. Actually, it was pretty funny. Charlie's tosses sucked. The first one didn't even reach the wall. The second was a creampuff, an underhanded toss tail-first against the wall.

"Okay, enough," Gus said.

He knocked on the Plexiglas then made a slicing motion across his throat with his right hand.

"Give it a whirl, Benny Boy," Gus said.

With that, I clutched my darts. I was afraid I'd prick myself and didn't look at my hand. Darts was never my bag. I tossed all three with quick snaps. Each one hit the wall with a ping, the second one dead center of a ticker symbol. It didn't matter which part touched. It counted. A bull's eye, on the first try, must have been dumb luck, but it still felt good.

I couldn't quite make out what Gus was saying behind the soundproof glass, but I saw his mouth curl into an O. When I pulled the second dart from the wall I noticed I'd hit the letter O, right in the hole. For some reason this made me flinch.

My monkey followed me to the wall and tugged my pant leg. I didn't hand over the darts till Gus tapped the glass. My monkey almost jerked them out of my hand. At least, it seemed that way. He made three quick chucks. Each landed within a close range, as if he were trying to hit the same mark. Two of them actually did.

When I escorted my furry friend out, Gus put his hand up blocking me from crossing the hall's threshold.

"You know, you'd be disqualified because you didn't set him behind the line."

"What?"

"They always need to stay behind the line," Gus said, "No exceptions."

I then looked down at the masking tape on the floor and shrugged my shoulders.

That night I dreamt of great apes, monkeys, and prosimians. I was a hominid trapped in a mud bath and the apes tossed stones, nuts, anything and everything at me; couple of them busy sharpening spear points. A whole pile lay there waiting for my nose as its bull's-eye. They picked them up and flung them at my head and when they cracked, egg dripped all over my face.

Woke up in a cold sweat. Took a hot shower with a brand new loofah sponge and scraped off dead and itchy skin.

Warming Up In The Bullpen

A smattering of macaques poked their heads under the desk. They ran amok. One with a jet black goatee chased after a spider monkey with his finger flush up his nose. Since the snow monkeys were unloaded into the bullpen the mood of the room swung in a new direction, lopsided by a thick sheet of testosterone.

I liked being stationed there. It made me feel better that they weren't always jailed in their tiny cells. For a while, both sexes were together. Then one day Malthus lost an eye and the females were pulled out. They made the move partly to protect the females, but also to keep the males in one piece. The males had a tendency to roughneck to impress the gentle sex.

I heard the great apes once had their fling with the dartboard, but it was much more difficult keeping them in line. Many grunts got mangled trying to keep orangutans and gorillas from making mountains out of molehills.

It was nothing like a zoo, more like a sitcom. Jasper, the itinerant elder baboon, perched on the rosewood desk as if directing a scene. With a deadpan gaze over his pesky comrades, swaggering from side to side, he squashed his hands together forming a tight fist. He shook his doubled fist with the zealousness of a high-stakes craps shooter. A cacophonous staccato ricocheted off the walls.

Jasper poked Thelonious, the reclusive snow monkey, who had been ruminating in the corner with his spoon. Jasper trapped the spoon so Thelonious wouldn't pling the mug he held. His passion was for playing music off cups, his cheeks, whatever he got his hands on.

Frankly, I understood his desire to be left alone to waddle in his thoughts, and I developed a certain affinity toward him. One moment he loafed in the corner, and then the next thing he'd up and do his best bongo medley on the file cabinet. I made a point of bringing him a new toy each time. His fingers were meant for more than darts, whereas the other monkeys reveled in the pointlessness of the pointy objects.

The room was stocked with peroxide and bandages and I was the nurse. The tradition passed down to each newbie. The funny part was that more bandages were wrapped in the bullpen while the monkeys warmed up, roughhoused. Paper cuts accounted for many of the casualties because they couldn't keep out of the file cabinets. Paper airplanes were a great warm up for them, but thus yielded numerous cuts.

Charlie arched his back as if mirroring Pancho's shuffle sling, a fruity throw the other monkeys mimicked. Surprisingly, though, Pancho had pretty good results. Charlie pumped his fist to show support for his monkey. And I brought a snack tray around of bananas, celery, pickles, and pumpernickel. Apparently, pumpernickel had become the bread of choice amongst the monkeys.

Thelonious picked the seeds out before he took a bite. He chomped the crust, tossing away the bread. The others scooped the middle into a ball and snacked, bouncing the crust off each others' heads. Thelonious nibbled on a seed.

"He's deadweight," Charlie said.

"What do you mean?" He's the nicest of the bunch. Never bugs anybody and you should really hear his rendition of "*Shoeless Joe from Hannibal Mo.*"

"Big deal. His stats are crap."

"He's finding his way."

"If he was a filly, they'd turn him into glue."

"And if he didn't groom your buddy Pancho over there what would he be chalking up? Let's not forget that. It's a thing called friendship. Ever heard of it? Once they feel shut out, isolated, they get depressed and can barely function. No sir, Thelonious is a good apple."

Thelonious hoisted his celery and flailed the stalk like a conductor's baton. His head tilted swaying to the music of Berlioz. Music streamed into the room a couple of days back. Berlioz, in fact. Thelonious was entranced. Music to sooth the savage beast. He didn't have the same level of glee with Haydn, Sibelius, or Shostakovich. With such a name as Thelonious you'd think his musical thirst would salivate for the discordant chords of the late Bop Piano King with the same moniker. Thelonious the monkey, Thelonious Monk, coincidence – I think not. But his passion split in two for both classical and show tunes.

Pancho snagged the celery from my snow monkey's grasp, tossing it to Benji, then to Nietzsche until Jasper intervened. It was monkey in the middle. Charlie slapped his knee he laughed so hard. Not me. I felt Thelonious's pain having been the monkey in the middle so many times myself.

Drop By Anytime

After work, I moonlighted with my bookstand hoping to see Luz again. This was the only way I seemed to come across her. Creeping into summer, I stretched my day till the moonbeams cast their glow. Brig visited me though. He, I could count on. I was pulling the tarp over my table just as the drops turned to drizzle. He sneered not able to find a single chess book. His puss swished tight as if sucking a lemon. He dug through his jacket, rattled change. The rain made his hair droop to the side.

"How are tricks?" he opened.

"Not too shabby. Been busy." I said.

"How's the monkey business?"

"Got some boomers."

"Good for you, dawg."

Brig grabbed the top of his head and chin at the same time and gave his neck a sharp twist until it cracked. Then he moved on to his knuckles.

"Tell you, I never looked at them the same. I rarely go to zoos now. Their just bigger jails."

"Well, at least I know if I'm keeping an eye on them they're okay."

"True that. Charlie, still there right?"

"Yup. He's a weirdo. I kind of like him."

"Takes one to know one."

My cheeks were wet. I snorted some water out of my nose and bagged up the rest of my books.

"Care for a friendly game?" Brigg asked.

"Here now?"

"We can duck into a coffee shop."

"What about Thompson Street?"

"Yeah."

"Two bucks an hour for a table."

"I'm not forking over any of my hard-earned stash. I've got my own board and pieces."

"Dude it's only a couple of blocks."

He unzipped his poncho and shook a little wooden box. On the bottom half corner it read *Made in the Philippines*. He primped it open and voila, instant chess. With calculated thrusts he set up the board in record time.

"Ready."

We sought refuge in the lobby of NYU computer center. It looked like it was under renovation, but that didn't matter we parked on the cold floor and played. In twenty seconds, Brig built a monster attack. Well guarded pawns, knights anchored on solid posts deep on my turf. My meager defense couldn't withstand his force. He launched his bishops at me like battering rams and formed a pawn gridlock that virtually handcuffed me. He made suicidal exchanges which I greedily accepted. It didn't take long before he boxed me in a corner. I could've sworn a nunchuck came screaming at my head when he sandbagged my queen with his knight.

***

A week into my foray with the monkeys Mungo dropped in, bubblegum prominent. Thelonious slapped his hands together. From my angle, it seemed as if he smashed the big boss's bubble. Mungo didn't find the antics the least bit amusing. As Thelonious began hooting and hopping Mungo fumed. His face reddened. Steam plumed from his ears.

"Dunk that fucker," Mungo yelled.

Gus entered with a bright orange life preserver. Thelonious kept snickering, but when Gus opened the life preserver, he fell back. Gus had trouble getting Thelonious to slip in. He flailed his arms as if drowning on the floor. The other monkeys gaped with solemn eyes. They stopped snacking. I swallowed back a wash of acidic pulp. I was inches from vomiting over my shoes, but didn't. Gus had finally nabbed the colicky snow monkey, and I stayed back watching my rage ebb into reticence.

"What's next on my agenda?" Mungo asked.

Lulu flipped through a pocket pad, crossed out a line then propped the gnawed pencil behind his ear.

"We've got to shake a leg or we'll miss the Opera," Lulu said.

"What's playing?"

"Don Giovanni."

"That's a stretch for Olga and good for us."

"Sure boss."

"Benny, shake a leg," Mungo said.

"Huh, me?"

"Yeah, you. You're going to come along."

As we passed the hall, I heard the whirl of bubbling water. I smelt the boozy fumes of industrial-strength chlorine. What a ruse, whirlpools and Jacuzzi, who could think of anything but the pleasure. Just how did the tickling bubbles torture? I didn't hear Thelonious whimpering and didn't see Gus, the room they were in was closed off, but I hoped it was Gus taking the bath rather than Thelonious.

Thelonious

He didn't have a zippy toss. And, sometimes he missed the back wall by a mile. He was totally erratic, but when he did hit with bull's eyes 3, 4, 8 in a row. His motion was crooked, a cross between a shot-putter's and an iconoclastic concertmaster. He stepped off the line to play music off his cheeks, bongoing a file cabinet.

Only in the bullpen music played in the background as a motivating device for the monkeys. Thelonious swooned, jived, strummed. He hooted a gruff staccato of notes. What came out of his mouth was clamorous, but in his head he was Berlioz. I was torn between naming him because I felt it fitting to christen him with a classical composer's moniker. Though jazz seldom spilled into the bullpen I decided my erratic, passionate snow monkey deserved the name of one of my personal favorite jazz pianists the late mad genius of Hard Bop. Thelonious Monk. I reasoned the discordant bongos and notes my furry friend employed paid glorious tribute to the Pannonica purveyor.

I let him do as he pleased free to botch tosses, make bulls' eyes, or play stride-style piano off the keyless desk. We made beautiful Muzak together.

It only took a plink here and there. We thwarted naysayers day in and day out. We put in results. Ticker symbols pegged by Thelonious shot up an astronomical 327% in one week alone. It dipped to 194% by week two, but his picks were trailblazing ahead of the pack. He had a wild penchant for penny stocks, including a bio-pharmaceutical company with a surefire cure for Lupus, a carwash franchise owned by the former NY Mets centerfielder, and other goldmines.

Call Me Crackerjack

The Opera house was packed. A svelte usher, gingerly handling programs,checked our ticket stubs and led us to our Grand Tier box. A couple of tomato-headed philistines, from the neighboring box, snickered at our getups. Lulu draped in a Yankees jersey and I wore an Atari T-shirt and cargo pants. I felt idiotic, but Mungo wouldn't let me go home and change or even buy a respectable collared shirt.

"Have some freaking balls," he said. "You can't let the whole world rattle your cage."

"Easy for you to say," I said, picking at my pouchy side pocket.

"It is. I say it and I mean it."

Mungo clearly the best dressed in our party had a black silk shirt with the top two buttons undone revealing a shock of peppery hair and a red double-breasted sport coat squeezed into his seat an overstuffed lawn jockey.

Lulu's eyes bulged when the conductor led the orchestra into the overture his nonplussed expression seemed to be expecting batting practice. Mungo, on the other hand, was a bona fide aficionado. He impressed me again with his boundless unorthodox eclecticism.

"Damn," he muttered, when a slip of paper slid from the *Playbill*.

"Boris Gulko is filling in for Renzo Favot," Mungo said biting his lower lip.

If it had been a replacement for Don Giovanni or the leading lady, I could see him being distressed, but it was for the supporting male, Don Ottavio. It was also hard for me to comprehend the lead being a Baritone while the number two was a tenor. But I was a mere tyro in Operatic matters. I'd been farmed on Broadway Shows as a kid, so the subtleties that made the grander musical form what it was were foreign to me.

Still, as big a buff as Mungo was he couldn't just enjoy the performance. He had to have a little action riding on it. Down below in the orchestra sat Artie Pinto in a well-groomed tuxedo. Artie had been a long-time buddy/client of Mungo's. Artie had been missing out on the boomers Thelonious had been raking in for me. Artie was a contrarian by nature who usually bet against Mungo's crackerjacks. In the past he rode both the upside and the downside gains. He had the smarts to choose the opportune moment and sold short, meaning he bet that the stock would drop in value and by doing so he'd clean up when the boomers went bust. I'd hit a pretty solid streak. Lulu, by accident, had mentioned my monkey was a bit erratic. Artie was close enough with Mungo to know that the monkeys were our true stock-pickers.

Apparently, Artie took his short positions too soon. He and Mungo had a few side bets on the evening's performance. Mungo predicted three missed notes or less. Artie picked five or more. Mungo bet that less than half the orchestra seats would offer a standing ovation. Lulu was a dynamo head-counter, which is why Mungo sprung for his tickets. Usually, the lower level attendees were quick to their feet. Those who sat in the nosebleeds were the toughest critics. Mungo and Artie had their biggest bet on the Balcony. Since Don Giovanni was considered Mozart's finest work, the true blue diehards would need perfection to give a standing ovation.

Mungo gave a thumbs down to Artie to which Artie replied thumbs up.

"What's that all about?" I asked.

"Artie thinks the balcony will give a standing ovation. What a nut. It would have to be a perfect performance.

"No way."

"Isn't it possible?"

"Sure, but I've got the kicker. Zerlina is on the rag. So she's taking muscle relaxers and Vicodin. Her voice will crack."

"How do you know all this?"

"Yours truly is her boyfriend."

When Leporello, Don Giovanni's servant, sung his aria "Notte e giorno faticar" Mungo shushed me. But, then he dropped comments shortly after Donna Anna chased a masked Don Giovanni out of her house. I followed along the Met Subtitles then turned it off. I wanted to immerse myself in the unfamiliar. I'd taken some Italian in High School, but besides "Io giocco a beisball"and "Ciao Bella," I was pretty much an imbecile with the language.

The acoustics were fine, but not what I'd expected. I wasn't a big concert person by any stretch: rock, pop, or classical. I preferred recordings though not for the pristine sound. In fact, I had a wild fondness for my old 33 vinyl of Billy Joel's "It's Still Rock n Roll to Me." When I was a kid, the scratchy parts stirred a wild passion in me and I imitated the Piano Man. Nowadays, the unblemished recording didn't fizz and fluff in my gut. I guess I felt reassured by the skipping needle. The unexpected edge of a concert was too much for me.

The first act closed with Don Giovanni accosted by the Ballroom's guests. The fink turned on his servant, pulling a sword at his neck, and the women Don Giovanni toyed with finally size him up for the snake that he is. Mungo's girlfriend, Zerlina the peasant girl, gave a breathtaking aria "Batti, batti o bel Masetto" – Beat me, oh lovely Masetto. Mungo actually seemed stunned. But, the second act was long and there'd be ample opportunity for botch-ups.

Not that I could detect it, but Don Giovanni didn't pull his weight in his finale, trio with Leporello and Commendatore. His counterparts made up for his lack of bravura. Zerlina was riveting. My novice ear tingled when she shared her scales. She received two bouquets from the east and west wings. Mungo bumped his knee squirming. The orchestra rose, then the Grand Tier, Family Circle, and the Balcony. Mungo wore a fat sulking pout, a kid who wasn't willing to sing happy birthday.

Artie waited down by the lobby; he offered to buy Mungo a glass of champagne, the good stuff, but Mungo declined. Artie clapped his palm around Mungo's back and told his buddy to forget about it. Mungo shook his head.

Lulu pulled a stick of gum out to share with the big boss. Mungo handed the stick to me. I bobbled it and picked it off the floor. The wrapper stuck to the gum. I dug my nails into the piece and ended up shredding the thing. I chewed to be polite.

We went for burgers. Artie had an affair to tend to and promised to take his buddy up on a rain check. We stopped at a dive bar in Midtown near Penn Station. Lulu paid the bartender and brought boilermakers and Buds over to the booth. The burger order had already been placed. I didn't even get the chance to give my preference for medium, a bit pinky inside.

"Well done is how we have it," Mungo said.

I didn't exactly think he'd eat his meat raw, but his insistence on getting one extra charred puzzled me.

"If you don't like it drown it in ketchup. I'm paying for the God damn thing."

I grabbed my Bud hating its bland, pissy flavor. I sucked it back like Theraflu.

"What do you want out of life?" Mungo said.

I admired the kidney-shaped urn across the bar. It was said the ashes of a longtime patron rested there. Not a bad way to spend the afterlife.

"Simple things," I said.

"If only there were. Then along comes the ex-wife grubbing alimony, child support, come over and clip my lawn, that sort of thing. Lulu can tell you firsthand."

"It ain't no picnic," Lulu reported, slugging back his beer.

"Tell me what interests you, fast cars, white sandy beaches, hula dancers fanning you, feeding you pineapple, pussy."

"Sounds great, but it's not the whole enchilada."

"I'm going to level with you, and I never do this, not with grunts anyway, but I think you're the real deal. Not just today's crackerjack. That's why I recruited you. They've known about you for years."

"Who?"

"The powers that be they know everything they need to know, but they only bother us when there's something in it for them. Money, vital organs."

"Sounds like you're talking from experience."

"Maybe I am. I got too big for my britches and then they wanted a piece of me."

"I thought you had everybody eating out of your hand."

"Things got a bit hairy. Now, I'm back on track. What I'm saying is this, there's lots of talent out there, but there's one you."

"Thanks."

"Don't let it go to your head because I'll knock it out."

"So what do you want with me?"

"Relax. Put your faith in me. Just give me your all."

"Fine, you've got it."

"I run these exhibitions. Sometimes cockfights, but I've got bigger fish for you to fry."

"Will I still be working with Thelonious?"

"You and that God damn monkey. The two of you could be butt brothers."

"We make a good team."

"You're a bit of a fruitcake, but you know what? I like you. Okay, you play with your monkey, once in a while. But you kick some ass on this new assignment."

"No sweat."

The burgers came and I did as Mungo suggested. I drowned my burger in ketchup.

Luz Returns

Tuesday afternoons have somewhat of a mystical quality for me. There's a Moody Blues song honoring that listless second day of the week that's always made me sort of melancholy. Makes me think of swaying trees, naked except for a few leaves, I imagine myself as one of those shriveled leaves just before it gets kidnapped by a sudden gust of wind. The Tuesday I saw Luz again made me see her smile in my oatmeal for weeks.

I was into my next phase. Mungo had business elsewhere, so Lulu was in charge of the sparring session. He waved over the next thumb-wrestling combo to an open hexagon. The stench was thick, a mélange of armpits and testosterone. It was only the first day of warm-ups. The thumb-wrestlers, both confined to wheelchairs, docked into the seven-by-seven rubberized mat waiting for them. A ref assigned to each mat set the wrestlers into duel-pronged elastic elbow braces so that they were bound to each other. Then their fingers were doused with baby powder.

The surroundings were nothing like the metal bench-clad arenas many of them had once battled in, but they needed the competition, the contact no matter how goofy it seemed.

Toward the back of the arena a gorgeous brunette entered. Her long soft hair fell over her right cheek. Her milky white skin was only visible from her left side. She walked with a quick, deliberate pace and wore a gardenia-patterned sundress ruffling down to her knees. I turned for a moment, and then a whiff of delicious berries spun me around. She was steps away from me and the incandescent light fixture, swaggering above, made the sheen of her skin glow. I was so fixed on her I'd been spun around again, this time by the hungry athletes. The wobbly trays in my hands would have ended up on the floor had it not been for the countering bursts of inertia from the thumb-wrestlers and their quick reflexes snagging salami sandwiches, pound cakes and other goodies from my trays. My fear of being mauled by the herd outweighed my fear of clumsiness, and indeed I was outweighed.

Wheelchairs or not, they'd squash me if they had the chance. No teasing during mealtime. Who would've imagined thumb-wrestlers working up such appetites? They really packed it away, meat, cakes, cardboard, a finger if it got in the way. One less thumb put them in better contention to take home the grand prize, not to mention the year's supply of pork rinds. Unlike the other wrestling forms, Greco Roman, turnbuckle-rocking, arm and sumo, thumb-wrestling catered to the crafty and in a way, though it seemed less of a sport and more of a lowbrow parlor game than the other more physical wrestling forms, it bore a more evenhanded element than the others. For example, a sumo wrestler pitted against a barroom arm-wrestler would be a categorical mismatch, whereas if they were thumb to thumb you'd have a fair fight.

This one was Mungo's new baby, a surefire success; it was going to squash any hopes for Frisbee, Twister, or Yahtzee comebacks that, rumor had it, were looming toward their respective second winds.

"Next time put it in a bucket," somebody said.

Then I got a full view of the brunette's face. It was Luz. As beautiful as ever, her perfect lips slightly parted, without a touch of lipstick, but luscious, I could've kissed her right there. She held a leather-bound planner and had begun to scratch something down while I was still marveling over the itty bitty birthmark under her right cheek.

"Somebody has to feed the fish," I said.

"You mean sharks," she replied, her head still down scribbling whatever she was scribbling. She picked a cheese cube off my shoulder, "Watch your fingers these gorillas will bite them off if you're not looking."

"Watch it, gorillas, especially lowlands, are peaceful primates. They wouldn't hurt a fly unless you took their baby or their salad."

She looked over with that don't get smart with me expression of hers, and she finally recognized me.

"I don't believe it," she said. "What the heck are you doing here?"

"Just needed a little, you know, change of scenery."

"I had this funny feeling I'd see you again," she said, slipping the pen inside her planner's leather flap.

"Really?"

"You've come a long way since those stuffed animals," she said.

"Yeah, well I've got to pay the bills. So what are you doing here?"

"Networking." She waved to Lulu. "This is going to be huge, but I guess you already know that. I'm always looking for the next hot thing."

"Say, I know this is out of left field, but what the hell, how'd you like to check out this underground Salsa Club?"

"You know how to Salsa?"

"Sort of."

"Underground sounds right up my alley. The thing is I have a friend in town."

"Well, my friend Charlie told me about the place so I'm sure he wouldn't mind being my wingman."

"Listen, my friend's a great catch. Charlie should jump through hoops."

"You know Charlie?"
"Who doesn't? You just tell him to be on his best behavior."
"No problem."

***

Before we picked up our dates, Charlie needed to get some service to take the tension off the first date jitters. We passed by the neon glow dripping off Annie's Nail Salon's canopy. Charlie wasn't impressed with the merchandise and suggested we get some service elsewhere. I'd cruised through the neighborhood with him before, waiting for him to finish taking care of business outside other nail salons.

You get more than manicures if you ventured toward Broadway after hours, underneath the 7 train. There were a few other nookie nooks in the general Queens vicinity, but around that Broadway/Roosevelt intersection was the best action. Some shrimpy Colombians would rush to your car and toss cards into the open window like Ninja stars that had the addresses of these late night nail salons. In turn we ended up referring to them as cigar bars. We couldn't just say we were checking out nail salons, we weren't fruit loops and people could probably figure out the kind of shenanigans we'd be up to venturing off to these late night establishments. So cigar bar became the perfect codeword, although we kind of overused it, unfortunately in mixed company. Occasionally, some chica we'd meet would push us to take her along, thinking we were heading to a legit cigar bar, they had become fashionable, cigar bars that is, a little played out, but let's just leave it at faux-fashionable, Club Macanudo for example. Most of the time we got off the hook, but there was always some pain-in-the-rump who just had to tagalong, once we even brought a chica into our kind of cigar bar, turned out she was into it. Go figure.

We followed the path of the 7 line and when we got near Seventy-fourth we nosed into the first open spot. We went to a dive tittie bar for a couple of beers. Charlie had this incredible knack for sniffing out dive tittie bars in addition to nail salons that offered off the menu specials. He left me by the bar to take care of his business in the backroom and, of course, I was out of singles so I had to drop a five for the skankiest dancer on stage flaunting her two-dollar g-string. She came over when they announced the next dancer and she sat on the stool next to me.

"Didn't you go out with Bubbles?" she asked me, playing with my lobe.

She reeked of rubber cement. Her face looked like a pepperoni pizza. Ugh. I trooped out of there and chilled in Charlie's car until he had finished, despite the fact that some roughneck types kept passing by to mull over Charlie's ride. I wasn't going back inside the bar and have that skank mess with me.

It was true I used to go out with a stripper named Bubbles. Sue me. I was desperate back then, not that I wasn't again, but I kind of wanted to put the past behind me. Things would be different. Charlie and I were really going to dance in a nail salon's underground basement, Salsa, Mambo and whatever else they played. We even had dates. I fished the baby bottle of cologne from my leather jacket and patted it onto my puckered cheeks.

Five minutes later Charlie appeared by the front door. I plowed over the seat, gearshift in my gut, to unlock his side. We peeled out, made a u-turn and carved through back alleys until we pulled up at the place. There was a careful procedure to get in, so we watched from the car. A few moments later the bouncer, sucking down beer in a paper bag, approached us, but was swayed toward a Beemer full of chicas booming Reggaetón. They were greeted by another bouncer with a finely coiffed mullet and were then escorted downstairs. The one in the purple halter was what Charlie referred to as a chimichanga a real no frills piece of ass with a little bit of tummy. The chubbier chicas worked harder, was the old boy's maxim.

Two minutes later our dates arrived. We got out of the car. Luz wore a snug-fitting top, revealing plump breasts, the glitter around her top's neckline caught part of the fluorescent glow of the neon sign above and, for a few seconds, my balance wavered. With each teetering step she took, it appeared she was hovering, an angel coming in for a landing. When she waved, a swelling rumbled in my pants. The outer traces of her eyelids shaded turquoise, matching her beaded necklace. Delicately, I picked at my trousers' fabric so as not to draw attention. They approached us and Charlie rapped at my ribcage, his usually pasty mouth damp with drool.

Luz took my hand and Marta, her amiga, clasped Charlie's as though they both had found lost puppies. They were both so sexy, but approachable, or maybe that was because we had everything set. Neither of us would've had the balls to go over to them even in the darkness of a club.

We went downstairs. In the pitch blackness of the alleyway a Doberman shot out at us, biting at the fence. Charlie bumped into Marta and she threw her arms around him. Charlie bit his lip as the Doberman buried a wet nuzzle onto his arm, through the fence's crack. Fortunately, we were at the foot of the entrance and the doors swung open. A wash of light blinded us and the music almost bowled us back.

The main room was full of dancers twisting, turning, and spinning with gusto. They were so good it was frightening and I was about the worst dancer in the world, which didn't seem to matter to Luz, in fact, amidst a room of salsa sultans she clung to me like one of those cute fuzzy, clip-on koalas. She teased me but loved my energy.

"Let me just say you are probably the worst dancer I've ever met."

"That does wonders for me, let me tell you."

"I'm serious. I really am, but there's something sexy in the way you approach it. Your face has such um – fuego," Luz said.

Marta grabbed me from behind and I could feel the heat of her breath on my neck and I wasn't quite sure but maybe also her tongue as well grazing my ear, but it was so loud, I was so drunk and everything unraveled there, spinning with unbridled ferocity.

Despite everything Charlie was a good camper. He struck out with Marta. She ended up with another guy, who, before long, was deep sea diving down her throat.

"Que tal flaca," I said to Luz, the extent of my Spanish.

She laughed so I knew I still had a semblance of charm, she would, in the very least, take pity on me.

"To tell you the truth I'm not too crazy about this music," Luz said. "In Mexico, they have something called cumbia. All my aunts and uncles and cousins love it. To me, it sounds like somebody sandpapering a floor, but it's popular. Have you been to Mexico?"

"I'm embarrassed to admit, only to Cancun," I said.

"You have to go Guanajuato. They say if you've never been to Guanajuato then you've never been to Mexico."

"And what do you think?"

"I think you should go to any part of Mexico except Tijuana. When the sand of Mexico seeps into your shoes, you will always, always long return."

"Are you from Guanajuato?"

"No, from Mexico City, but I have been there. Actually, I haven't been to most parts of the country except for some of the provinces north and south of the city, Pachuca, Guanajuato, Acapulco. Once I even went as far down as Oaxaca."

"I took a Rise of Mesoamerican Civilization class a few years back, we studied the Mayans, the Aztecs and the ones with the giant football helmets."

"Giant football helmets?"

"The Olmecs, they had those huge heads that looked like helmets permanently emblazoned onto their heads."

"Don't tell me you're one of those assholes who compare everything to American pastimes."

"I don't even like football."

"Good, because the only real futbol is ours."

"I know you invented it, but the stakes back then meant your head on a platter."

We got back up to dance. Just as well, I got the sense that my charm had worn off. I was reminded of what an ex-girlfriend once told me that I was perfect until I opened my stupid mouth. That's when everything went south. She didn't get me.

Luz danced to my stuttering beat. She didn't seem to mind. She moved my arms like she were stringing along a marionette, the trouble was my feet couldn't keep up.

"You're amazing," I said, trying to keep pace with her rocking salsa steps.

"I wanted to be a prima ballerina," Luz said. "Believe it or not when I was a kid I danced for a professional company. You name it I did it, jazz, tap, ballroom. I still have a pair of my old slippers. My mother wanted to bronze them for me, but I wouldn't let her. Really silly of me, I thought she just wanted to crush my dream. I wanted to keep those slippers the way they were so that if the chance ever came back I could dance again."

Luz turned and walked away and I followed her. She stood by the wall, fanning herself.

"My dad keeps a whole bunch of old baseball scorecards from my Little League days," I said, "Sometimes he shows me them and tells me that he thought I could've been the greatest baseball player in the world and, I don't know, but it makes me feel lousy. I mean the guy's cracked if he thinks I could've been a Bambino. It makes me feel like shit that I led him on, thinking I could've been a great ballplayer. He's just an old fool."

Luz clutched my elbow.

"Don't you say that," she said. "You should respect him, he's your father. Someday you'll regret it."

Marta snuck up on us, perfect timing, yanking on my ponytail. Deeply I dove into Luz's brown eyes, swirling in them, hoping she would rescue me. Marta dragged me away, but I gazed at Luz. My body was going one way, but my attention was drawn to her, with a forceful almost magnetic undertow.

Luz looked off when Marta's fingers roamed my back, my feet miserably flubbing the beat as a maze of marvelous dancers glided passed us. I was humbled. Still, I threw everything I had onto that dance floor including the monkey, the pony and a little James Brown. I was going down swinging, the gringo that thought he could.

Turns out that many chicas enjoyed my comical act, Marta pulled me closer.

"Forget her, she's no fun. Believe me, I've been out with her. She's a prude," Marta said, bobbing her head so that her scoop neck revealed the better half of her goods.

"But you're friends," I said.

"So, I know how she is. Loosen up, let's have fun," she said puckering her lips.

All I could think of was that her mouth, which stunk like ashtray, had swapped spit with at least two other chicos that I had seen. Where was my dignity in all of this? Her thigh rubbing up against my crotch nullified whatever reasoning was percolating in my head and she grinned each time she felt a knock against her jeans.

A mature woman, in tiger-print pants, who from this point will be referred to as Tiger Pants, cozied up to me while I hadn't been paying attention. Marta and she took turns and every once in a while I stole a glance from Luz who was already dancing with a handsome fellow in a bandless collared shirt which she just so happened to unbutton.

Cheaper cologne, even more pungent than mine, fumed from Tiger Pants' sweaty neck. Her beer gut bopped against me reminding me of the heating pad I sometimes slept on whenever I had a really bad backache. Then she took my hands, gluing them to her rump. I'll be honest I was scared because Marta herself gave me the dirtiest look.

I felt like a heel and berated myself for losing Luz. Her graceful gliding steps, her charismatic flair; the way she scolded me for denigrating my father. She wasn't being feisty. She was being true to herself, spirited. Her magical aura filled the room, each step soft and graceful accentuated by her posture. She was elegant, the Latina Audrey Hepburn.

Though I lulled at the site of her sensuous legs and the ease with which her hips swayed, I kept returning to her previous concern about respecting my father. She hadn't met the man but spoke so passionately. I fixed on her dancing till she was blotted out by her partner's arm as he raised hers to spin her in the other direction. Then Tiger Pants pinched my cheek and I was forced to moon over her pimply face.

Move Over Bacon

The fat hand rolled past three when I had finally ditched Tiger Pants; she needed to freshen herself up in the ladies' room so I broke for the exit. Three-o-seven was my best guesstimate, watchless as always. I am constantly at the mercy of wall clocks, but I consider myself an excellent time-telling marksman once I have a frame of reference. An hour earlier, I had stolen a glance from somebody's wristwatch the last I had seen Luz. I would've said goodbye to her if she were somewhere in sight, but I couldn't risk Tiger Pants mugging me by the exit.

I grabbed the first taxi. No sooner did I open the door, Luz darted passed me and into the seat.

"Let go," she said, while I was still holding the door.

"C'mon let me at least take you home," I said.

"Fat chance. Why don't you go home with Marta?"

"I don't want her."

"Oh, that's a shame. I never would have guessed with the way you were slobbering all over each other."

"Hey, I didn't kiss her. She was the one who kept putting the moves on me."

"Poor baby. You think I'm stupid? You struck out so now you want your turn with me. Get lost."

"You're making a complete mistake. I can explain. Let's grab a bite somewhere and before you know it we'll be laughing about the whole night."

Then, as if I wasn't even standing there, the tall fellow, her dance partner with the swivel hips, slipped between us. Luz got out of the cab and let him press both his hands on her waist then locked lips. The driver honked and without giving it a second thought I jumped in the taxi and sped off. No more than five turtle steps and we missed the light. Luz pounded on the window, staring at me with wide, wet eyes. So I let her in. I wasn't sure what to say. I had done enough and felt stupid. Garbled apologies percolated in my head, none sounded sincere. But I wanted her. From the moment we danced, my sweaty hand fit perfectly in her grasp.

There was something different about my attraction to her. Yes, it was physical, but there was also this magical undertow, as though she pulled me back into my past unleashing the wholesomeness reminiscent of the crushes I had on the girls from elementary school before I gravitated toward the dizzy thrum of autoerotic pleasure. There was this tension in me. I wanted her, but wanted to prolong wanting her. Associating Luz with my childhood may have sired an unrequited lust for the girls I never consummated with, but it also grounded me in the past, which is perhaps why my feelings felt more juvenile, more obtuse.

Now, my friends had teased me that I had a thing for Latinas, which was part myth, part truth, but there were one or two Latinas from my past that I had unhealthy crushes on, but never did anything with even though I had lit entire rows of church candles so that my fantasies could have been realized.

There was this one girl, Sara Gonzalez, who I had the deepest puppy love for, back when I was thirteen. I used to pluck soda can pull-rings to her initials. S was too far to twist a pull-ring before it snapped off so I settled for G.

We played in the parking lot across from our school. That's where the gang from Our Lady of Perpetual Hope, Mercy, and our public school friends hung out. Sara was in the grade below me. For some reason, her class got let out a bit earlier than mine. By the time I made it outside she'd already be over by the wall slapping a handball, sitting on the bike rack doodling in her notebook, always there, a given.

This one time the two of us were knee deep into a game of hide and seek snuggled atop of one another below the convent steps across from the school. The Sisters' wet clothes hanging out to dry over the laundry line above us, our protective canopy: an aquamarine jogging suit, red and white, green and white tube socks, a couple of turtlenecks and of course a trio of dangling habits. Father O'Grady pointed out this eyesore as a way to get parishioners to give more during collection time. So help me, he went as far as to say that the nuns had themselves an underground laundry business to get new textbooks for the school. It was one of the best hiding spots because it was sunken in and also because most kids were too chicken to get caught there by one of the nuns.

Sara and I didn't want anybody to see us because then we'd be out of the game but more importantly, if the kids saw us together some rumor might break out that we were boyfriend and girlfriend. I was mortified not knowing what the hell to do. My skin was itching with desire, itching with grief, her warm, sweet breath blowing in my ear; I wanted to take the initiative but didn't know how.

We held each other for quite some time, her silky chestnut hair tumbling in my face. I was practically munching on it, the yummy scent of strawberries, her breasts flush against my arm. I longed to taste her glistening lips as she moistened her tight pink mouth with the smooth blade of her tongue, but we kept our hands to each other's backs, playfully stroking the grooves of each other's spine but there was nothing more.

Nobody ever found us that afternoon and I was upset, thirsting for that magical spark that a rumor could ignite. I was so damn passive.

In the taxi, sitting with my leg kissing Luz's thigh, we hit a pothole and I had the very same feeling I had as a child on the steps with Sara. I yearned to wake up next to Luz spooning her sensuous curves, but was again too frightened. The moment passed by the time we got to her crummy walkup.

She beat me out of the taxi. I paid the driver and left a two dollar tip because I needed to catch up with Luz before she slammed her door in my face.

"Look, I was a real jerk," I said.

"Yes, you were."

"But I am harmless. All thumbs. A pretty girl flirts with me and I'm putty."

"You are nice, Benny. But I think we're better as friends."

"Fine."

I think she was surprised I agreed so fast. Truth is, it was out of nervousness. She dropped her guard and we stopped at a nearby diner to split a plate of fries and mozzarella sticks.

We grabbed a window booth; the pliable plastic cushions scattered with our predecessors' mess. She filched a wad of napkins from the clunky dispenser and wiped down her seat casting her cold, sparkling brown eyes on my wide, sweaty collar. The blushing pink glow of dawn swept through the cloudy glass. I was happy nothing happened with Marta, not that I couldn't have used a fling, but I wasn't ready to give up on Luz just yet. If friendship was all it would be I could take it, for the time being. For too long, I'd consigned myself to the role of mook who had nothing but a souvenir pair of panties, who cried in his beer to other mooks who had nothing but souvenir panties.

The thought crossed my mind, Luz, with the other fellow. The way he so brazenly stepped between us, planting one on her right there. I imagined them having done so much more, but I didn't mention it, why dig up muck. She'd only accuse me of indulging her trampy friend and Tiger Pants.

Luz chuckled at my corny jokes; it sent goose pimples down my legs. She wasn't trying to be nice; she appreciated stupid humor. It was refreshing. The tough part was staring across the boulevard at the Eight-ball Motel where I used to take Bubbles after she finished pole-dancing. If Luz only knew? For a moment, I worried that Bubbles might sneak up behind me pressing her Oil of Olay hands over my eyes. Luz wasn't going to believe she was my cousin that's for sure.

Luz tried to make an origami pelican from a napkin. It looked more like a torpedoed submarine. She chewed with such tiny bites, they were practically anti-bites they were so small, but it fascinated me the way she hid her mouth. I looked away so as not to make her feel uncomfortable, but had this sort of goofy grin every time I peered out at that flea-bag motel.

"What?" she said, "Are you laughing at the way I'm eating."

"Who's laughing?" I said, frosting the window with my breath. "Just thinking, any harm in that?"

"No, but you're thinking too loud, with too much smirk. My father used to say that to my brother, when he was up to no good."

"Believe me I'm just having stupid thoughts."

"Tell me."

"It's nothing, really."

"You must have ships bottled in you. I can tell you're one of those types who thinks and thinks to himself, then puff, squeezes out a ship whenever the need comes along. And then you tell anybody, but seldom those who you're really close to. Am I right?"

"Would you like to be my analyst, bartender?"

Luz sank back into her seat. She didn't look my way though I leaned in. She kept her eyes down.

"If you must know," I said, "Sometimes it takes this so-called stranger to awaken something in you. Least it does for me."

"But you can't keep things from those who love you. You need to tell them," she said.

"Look, I don't know what impression you're getting of me, but I'm not a hermit. So maybe I've only really opened myself up a few times, no sane people gush themselves out all the time. As a kid I wore my heart on my sleeve, but I got cautious with age."

"Me, too, but I get this feeling you've always been a bit cautious and I think it has a little to do with your mother, how she never let you keep your bedroom door closed."

"I told you that?"

"It seems to me that you probably revealed a lot in your childhood and now you're choosy sharing your personal life which is why you'd rather talk about philosophy, wine or other non-threatening topics."

"But you love Italian wine, too. And besides I made a good point earlier that a nice crisp Falanghina would cut through these grease-clad fries."

"Joke if you want, but you need to ask why you keep things to yourself. And more importantly, why you wanted to share with me?"

"Does it matter if I have the right words? That's nonsense anyway. Look, I know it might have been the booze talking in me earlier, but I'm sober now."

"Yeah and?"

"I'd rather be here with you sharing fries then with –"

"I got it."

"But let me finish."

"I know where you're going."

"So then let me go there."

"It's not necessary."

"Listen to yourself. You're telling me to get the ship out of me and you stop me short. Damn it let me bring it into the harbor."

Luz stood abruptly. This time she wouldn't let me take her home, but she dropped a twenty for the snack.

***

When I woke up the next day, I was shrouded underneath a pile of laundry and a note written by my mom that said if I was still going to live a frat boy's lifestyle I was better off getting a place of my own. Really, it was about time. I was closing in on twenty-nine.

There was a bowl of sliced fruit and a corn muffin waiting for me in the kitchen, but I was too hung over to think about anything but paying homage to the porcelain potty. As the day dragged on and as the booze wore off, I was back to my usual self, indecisive, circumspect and calculating. I brooded over things I said to Luz. The things I might have, could have, and wasn't sure I had said. You never know what kinds of judgments somebody makes about you no matter how they smile, smirk, or snarl. You try to look at the whole thing objectively, but at some point panic takes over, this is when you know you have feelings or are developing feelings for somebody and you fret over all the permutations of things they can imply from what you said or didn't say.

While I hadn't told her anything outlandish, my tendency to take sponge baths slipped out too easily. Why did it matter anyway, it wasn't as if we exchanged numbers or anything, we traded emails. It was the harmless way to tell somebody you just wanted to be friends. She even said we ought to keep it friends. Now I did know where she lived, but who in their right mind would show up by somebody's building unannounced. It was the kind of thing you saw in a made for T.V movie or heard stories about an ex-lover stalking behind the bushes, but it

53

wasn't something I did so I washed my hands of the matter preparing to start another week of the same old grind so what was the sense of torturing myself over what could have been.

I should've learned from my past mistakes, but as Luz said, I had ships bottled inside me. Instead of confronting my mother after the photo clipping incident I called her Auntie for a whole year. I suspected her of deliberately sabotaging my stake in Playmobiles. Indian headdresses, knight breastplates, fire helmets had been all missing for a while. I figured little by little she was erasing me; first my pictures then my toys. For spite, I called her Auntie. One day while she dug through the garbage, the corners of her mouth shriveled up, the cleft on her chin deep, as if I'd cut her denouncing her motherhood; I felt guilty and decided to call her Mom again.

Not long after that, I saw her with a box of old photos. I heard her talking to Dad about how much she hated her hairstyle in some of the old pictures. Turns out she was only snipping out her ugly shots, when she still donned her Doctor Zira-do, which came about after letting a neophyte hairdresser talk her into the then, hottest cut in town. PS, the disappearing Playmobile accessories were found after we'd had the plumber come by to unclog the pipes, it seems I hadn't accounted for the possibility of losing my cherished accessories during the underwater expeditions I'd been sending my little men on. Certainly, I wasn't so careless.

Nonetheless, for a whole year because of that silly Auntie thing, my mother and I, shall we say, had strained relations, which may have prolonged that whole oedipal baloney from making its natural progression.

It takes altricial mammals longer to mature than precocial mammals as it is but that misjudgment on my part set my development back. I don't blame anybody but myself and chance. For if I believed this whole shebang called life was totally designed by a solo architect I wouldn't be so keen on all the possibilities. I would take my fortune cookies at face value. Those hailstorms, earthquakes and whatnot have to be the byproduct of too many self-indulging prayers that the poor overworked, non-union gods can't figure out which to grant first. Lines of prayer cross pitting the gods into a reality television style competition. When they lock horns, watch out.

Now, as a proud disciple of pragmatics I brood over chance. It's nobody's fault it took me so long to clear the hurdle of that great big philosophical juggernaut, fate. Truth is I wished I could still believe we lived in the kind of world where the red carpet would eventually roll out to my assigned destiny. That would take some of the pressure off all the brooding I did over chance. I just couldn't look myself in the mirror and pretend that's the way it was.

It was nice to know my mother still put the time and effort into preserving the family tree by way of pictures, which I'd grown rather tired of looking at, but especially of hearing about, little me, in our pictures. Just for laughs I might throw an Auntie at her here and there and she was usually fine with it, although with company around, she usually waited until they were gone before twisting my ear.

The door to the living room was slightly ajar so I slipped in without causing a commotion. Mom was in the midst of putting up new pictures atop the hutch that, until that afternoon resided by the other end of the room. The walls, though sanded and whitewashed, more or less remained the same.

Just for thrills, I drummed my knuckles along the door as the cuckoo clock clucked five chimes, drowning out my soft tap, tap, taps. Then I wiped my glasses with the bottom of my T-shirt. The faces in the picture might as well have been fifty-watt bulbs or faceless Potato Heads. Impaired vision paralyzes you. You constantly mistake people, and gender becomes obscured. It's a cost effective way to haze through life without having to plunk down big bucks for designer drugs.

Not until I planted my glasses on my nose was I able to see. With the stereoscopic boost, I discovered who the werewolf and the pirate in that picture were – none other than my childhood friend Prem and myself. The hairy-masked Prem was in the process of sprouting horns above my three-corner-hatted head though this was almost indiscernible because I was giraffing my neck so I wouldn't have to suffer the embarrassment of those fingered horns whisking through posterity.

What has bothered me for so many years is that I am never sure about the memories I have regarding certain pictures. Especially the ones regarding those nebulous years, you know, when you are small and everybody from your family, your aunts, uncles, and cousins flog you with what they remember of you back then, when you couldn't care about anything in the world but stuffing your fat face seven layers into your birthday cake.

Now, by sight I know how old I was in any photograph. I know what year it was taken and all that useless malarkey, but I cannot precisely recall when the photo was snapped. In other words, I have become so used to flipping through family albums that I recall what people have said about such and such occasion. That in turn becomes my memory.

What has happened to that personal, sensuous record of time that only belonged to me? Did it too get sucked down some wormhole where all the intergalactic dust, sock puppets, pen tops and all those other things that Saint Anthony couldn't locate have fallen?

Thumbs Up

This next part really could not have been anticipated. It all started when I returned to the arena. While I was carting another batch of hulks around in wheelchairs, Lulu pulled me aside for some late-breaking news. My arms were aching and my brows were dripping with sweat. He gave me the sports section to dab myself off.

"Mungo wants you to spar," Lulu said.

"Whoa!"

"Don't make a big deal. Who knows for how long?"

So what? The big guy thought enough to keep me from grunting and stretch my thumb-span into the hexagon. My cagy combination of brains and beauty was just the glue to keep the new following of saps into Mungo's new baby.

You could say he was sort of a mensch to those poor, washed-up slobs who couldn't body slam or land a dropkick. Former wrestlers, kick-boxers and nefarious street fighters were welcome to enter the competitions so you can see how neatly I fit into the picture. I was the perfect underdog.

It wasn't as if I'd get pulverized by any of the giants, many of whom were gimps by now. All I did was step in to the hexagon, last a few minutes and collect a paycheck. Quick, painless and profitable. Okay so I was getting ahead of myself. Mungo wasn't letting me grab a piece of the action. I still was working for peanuts. But, I took a huge step up the ladder from grunt to goober. Frankly, as long as I could stay in this part, maybe get a bump in pay, I'd be dandy. The only thing that worried me a little was the kind of transfiguration needed to morph me into a goon, but I figured I'd worry about that later.

My former co-working grunts, if you'll pardon the pun, became disgruntled when they saw me locked in battle during the competitions. Charlie watched with a gloomy puss as I prepped for my first bout with Sven Bergstrom, a former pro wrestler from Sweden. Charlie and I really hadn't spoken much after our date with Luz and Marta. I got the feeling he was avoiding me. He tucked his arms to his chest as if waiting for some kind of apology.

I kept my wits tethered to the task ahead, Sven Bergstrom, two-hundred mostly solid pounds of muscle outhulked my lithe one-fifty frame. They called him the Big Cat, because once upon a time, before his knees were jelly, he'd leap off the top turnbuckle then flatten you out with a flying body press. He also had this vise-like grip called 'The Claw.'

He held you up by the face with your feet dangling off the ground. Now he duked it out with thumbs, but don't get me wrong, he wasn't any slouch. Even with the limited thumb-wrestling repertoire he was one helluva competitor.

Sven had a calm demeanor, his head dipped to the side and his eyes never blinked, almost glued in their slit-like position. You weren't sure if the guy was dozing off or squinting, but he had lightning fast reflexes. A lot of good it did him, confined, as we all were, to the rubberized mats. There was no raised ring as in boxing or pro wrestling. No stools that you might find for a barroom arm-wrestling duel. Once you stepped onto that rubberized mat the match started. If, for whatever reason, one foot stepped off you were disqualified. This made for some interesting tactical play, in which competitors tried psyching each other out with head fakes, arm-thrusts, twists and curls. Move an elbow as long as you didn't twist your opponent into anything that resembled wrestling holds.

The setup provided intimacy. Everything was ground level. One might have the urge to tickle a competitor, but this didn't happen. A dozen or so fans loitered by each mat, no seats, not even those foldable metal jobs. At any given time, there might be one hundred people in the entire arena, including thumb-wrestlers and trainers. Mungo kept it cozy. According to him, crowd control fostered talk and word soon spread. It's the same way with new, exclusive hotspots and rare baseball cards. People want what they cannot have. It may have something to do with the inferiority complex gene.

Lulu stood in my corner holding a bucket of chalk so I could get a double dip. When I pulled my hands out I was wearing two brand new white gloves. Lulu chopped at the back of my neck and shoulder blades in the general trapezius region to loosen me up.

Most of the crowd was composed of competitors; some had been cut loose from the roster and were hoping to fill-in for whomever. My bout was more of a test run. Should I fair well I might get another crack at it. Mungo hadn't quite made up his mind yet.

"You never said it was going to be a sudden death match," I quibbled.

"Fugeddaboutit," Lulu said, trying to calm me.

I thought I'd have, in the very least, a two out of three falls match. It had been ages since I'd done any serious thumb-wrestling. You just didn't find pickup games the way you used to nowadays. Some of the kids from my old school, Our Lady of Perpetual Hope, used to play for quarters outside the rectory. Losers treated at the arcade.

This was a whole different ball of wax. It was scary and exhilarating. Call me nuts but the idea that I could be competitive again gave me an unbridled rush I hadn't had in years not since I'd hung up my cleats and baseball bat. I needed to prove myself.

"If I do well I'll get another shot right?" I said.

"Nope," Lulu said.

"What do you mean nope?" I said. "I thought it was a given."

"Don't you worry just take care of business."

"Lulu, you're killing me."

With that he gave me a smack on the rump, the force sent me onto the designated mat. Sven was all set to go. We squared off as the bell rung. Sven smothered my fist, he could've squashed me but somehow my thumb was nimble enough to dodge and parry. No sneak attacks allowed for this event, when you shoot the index finger out for a cheap pin. This was hardcore. Two other bouts were going on simultaneously. Most of the crowd swarmed around Bald Bull scrimmaging with the perennial underdog Glass Joe. He had what they referred to in the sport, as a glass thumb. He blistered easily. He'd dislocated himself numerous times and made losing an art. Fans cheered for him with ubber zeal rallying for him as much as for themselves lusting for David to upend their respective Goliaths, whatever they were. Glass Joe owned a hotdog stand a couple of blocks from Madison Square Garden. He rarely won but always put on a good show, which is why Mungo didn't need another Glass Joe in the house. Maybe it was stupid to glance at his match every so often, but I couldn't help it.

He and Bald Bull were rocking. In fact, I had the opportunity to catch the start of their duel. Bald Bull rubbed my head for good luck. It probably should have been the other way around, but I wouldn't deny the musclehead.

From the thundering hooray, I knew Glass Joe had made a pin and I foolishly turned to catch a glimpse only to see Bald Bull had broken loose. Sven was furious I'd looked away, his mouth twisted in anger. Purple lines flexed to the surface of his forehead. He jerked my arm and it felt as though he'd yanked it right out of its socket. He had managed to wrap me in some kind of pretzel hold, which wasn't exactly kosher, but my limber thumb bobbed, even with my arm pinned behind my back. No matter how hard he tried, he couldn't pin me. His whole face purpled squeezing me with gargantuan oomph; his sunken cheeks seemed to be sucking down an infinitely long spaghetti strand. Luckily for me the Big Cat stepped off the mat and was disqualified.

Mungo saw everything. He didn't exactly smile but didn't sulk either. A bunch of the thumb wrestlers stopped to congratulate me. It was sort of cool, but I needed to pull a legitimate pin.

Two days later I did.

Mungo let the crowds bloom. Overnight we'd gone from roughly one-hundred attendees to two-thousand. Then we changed locations to septuple that number. It was high time for him to start cashing in; plus I'd built quite a fan base. They waved foam thumbs in my honor.

Bald Bull continued rubbing my head for good luck each fight. As corny as it sounds, I really started to enjoy the cheers. Just hearing my name chanted gave me a rush. Wasn't quite the same as being a rock star, but damn close. I'd caught up on all those squandered years when jocks ruled the roost, even though my event fell into the dinky category, not quite Olympic-proof.

The steady adulation spoiled me.

Next I faced Grouper who earned his name because he used to whack his opponents on the back of the noggin with a wet one right from the bucket filled with tuna, mackerel, and flounder. Oh, and his fleshy face pouched like the aqueous Serranidae of the subfamily Epinephelinae, Grouper to the layman. He'd been the cat's pajamas north of Poughkeepsie, mainly a Greco-Roman tumbler who also excelled in Drunken Monkey Kung Fu. He suffered from a worsening scoliosis situation and when he was seen slipping on his trusty back brace he was lampooned all the way to Potsdam. Any further north and he'd be shunned to Canada.

His grip wasn't too bad, but it felt like he'd rather shake hands than squash my thumb. I coiled around his thumb and created my own handy version of the camel clutch throwback and homage to the Iron Sheik. Boy did it work. Grouper pooped out and the ref raised my hand in victory.

I hardly had the chance to savor the win when a new path cleared for me to tangle with Slippery Slim. He'd earned his reputation for greasing himself down before each contest so he could easily slip from a pin.

To make matters worse Slippery Slim had hitch hiker's thumb, so it was a pipedream to wrap your thumb around his, since his thumb dipped back as far as it did, a double-jointed banana. Combined with his greasiness, he'd been considered nearly impossible to beat, what with thumb-wrestling's equivalent of the spitball, and no bunt to counter it – that I knew of then.

The packed arena waved foam thumbs. The two earlier matches hardly served as appetizers for the restless crowd. The electricity was pumping. I recognized the old woman I'd seen the other day tackling the Indian man over by the Plex's man-made waterfall, this time sans walker. She punched her fist into her hand as I struggled to get better leverage on my opponent.

She screamed, "Kill 'em" at the top of her lungs, shaking me in my boots, but if that wasn't enough she tossed some kind of foreign object at

Slim, maybe it was a doorknob. Whatever it was it took Slim off guard; I was mucho indebted to her impeccable timing. Slim flinched and felt the back of his head. I'm not sure if he really got conked or if he was merely startled, but I slid in for the pin. His knuckle crackled and I pressed him for a three count.

The next day I picked a flyer off the street marked with a fresh stamped shoeprint. The ad showed, presumably, my thumb draped in some kind of mass-produced kid's fruit roll-up snack. The closer I inspected the image the more apparent it became that it was my thumb in question and not some stand-in model. My left was naturally less robust than my right 1) by stroke of the old genetic wand and 2) on account of the baseball that plunked me right on my nail during a batting cage incident that occurred in the Age of Little League. Never grew back so well.

The picture had the appropriate indentation if you looked at it under a microscope, and believe me I took the liberty, so I knew it was my image they were capitalizing on, and not some thumb model filling in my place. Let's just say that was the case anyway, they still would have been exploiting me, but who was I going to turn to. For all I knew Mungo was the brainchild behind this ad campaign. If I confronted him he'd pat me on the back, bore me with another dyspeptic story about apple-picking, by which time he would have squirmed out of any distasteful mentioning of my royalties.

I had come a long way since childhood when the kids anointed me the fifth grade brainiac. Somebody once stuck a lump of clay into a mayonnaise jar and put it on my desk, which I found utterly stupid, what with the smoothness of the clay and the lack of folds it was a poor substitute for the globulous gray matter. The more I stewed over the sterile quality as the lump lay there, the queasier I got.

Then I had a flashback to my first encounter with Mungo and my naked lobe beaming on the giant screen in Mungo's office. It hit me then that for all the pubescent nonsense I went through, I never once got crowned for my achievements at any science fair.

Noble Rot

Long before the thumb-wrestling, the dart-slinging monkeys, long before Mungo and even Luz, I started to notice my memory waning. Which made it all the more ironic that I got sucked into this new world, on account of my great memory. There were more impressive specimens who had memorized monstrous streams of numbers, take that guy for instance, who went through the twenty-seven hour ordeal of rattling off Pi to the one millionth decimal place. My gift was tame by comparison. Mine was on the decline. I waxed over the same names and passages, as if I had hit a saturation point. Whatever clogged in my head had no escape hatch. I was grateful Mungo had me doing something mechanical, it kept me from dwelling on my mortality.

I heard that certain smells awaken memories. If you take a deep whiff of a scented candle or a plastic baggy brimming with pungent herbs the synapses rapid-fire. It might trigger a thought and let you bolden the lines around a blurry picture from the past. Is this the typical affliction a young person worries about? No. Wasn't this more the domain of stroke victims and those petering toward Alzheimer's? Sure, yet I found myself chartered to this frightening place.

I'd been leafing through a soiled book on wine-making. Bred on soda, the taste of wine never really appealed to me. The pictures were pretty crappy, but the verbiage and the descriptions intrigued me. I started perusing other wine books: snob editions, the history of Bordeaux, tasting journals. Each time I read a new one I circled back to the same things, words.

Wine and words sparked my curiosity. I couldn't get enough and I had a scientific mind from all that anthropology I'd loaded up on.

Naturally, I had to put myself to the test and partake in wine tastings. The pundits grappled with meaning as if planning to squeeze quiddity from grapes. One wonk claimed he recalled the distinctive aromas and flavors of more than fifty thousand different wines. Once, a big-time beer guzzler he'd grown bored of his barleycorn brew and took to wine. He didn't even like the taste, but approached the whole thing scientifically. This gelled with me. I too, wanted to prove I could discern minute variation blindfolded and baffle judges time and again with my tasting prowess.

Wine was fine to read about but unless you drank the damn thing it didn't really leave its impenetrable stain on you, so to speak. I checked out free wine tastings for kicks. They were everywhere, so long as you knew where to find them. There were so many quaint little shops and the turnover was huge. Many places went out of business before I even had the chance to make a visit. That's how it was, the old standbys thrived. Those marked my swigging grounds. Eventually, I went to the tastings with a religious devotee's fervor.

Wine was booming since the mad scientists, known to the cognoscenti as enologists, had tweaked the right flavor for the American palate and by consequence the Americanos, me included, had gotten smitten with the randy grapes, riding the wave of, dare we call it, the international style. So many golf-checkered-trouser types piddled their way into these events leering at the free, half-poured samples. I had my own uniform; a ribbed sweatshirt, or turtleneck and a pair of cords.

Forget the Riedel or the Spiegelau goblets, hand me a Dixie Cup. Give me the unusual, the variety nobody has heard of that upon first sip leaves your buds bitter and brooding. It's a bit of mental judo I prefer brooding over grapes than having them brooding on my tongue. Gathering the real substance of the grape has to do with the weight and the pulse, as though it were living and breathing. And so they are.

The Grog Shop had some of the best tastings, in my humble opinion, the most expansive selection. Sometimes they offered the old standbys, Burgundies, Rhones, Barolos, but they also stocked the obscure. They carried all the former Soviet Satellite wineries canoodling with the European Union pushing their garage-pressed concoctions. That's why I was a regular at the Grog Shop. They couldn't give a rat's ass how snooty you were. They didn't sell cases by the bulk you had to handpick what bottles you wanted. Mainly, you bargained when they pulled in new treats or they felt insulted. In fact, I even bartered with them, occasionally with books. Sometimes I traded stuff that Brig gave me from his scavenger hunts.

So for me the Grog Shop was another one of those stops I considered a home away from home. They catered to nothing and nobody, never twisted your arm into buying their crap, always allowed you the freedom to meander through the aisles. Break a bottle and they mopped it, but not before everybody nearby had a chance to sniff. Never had the pleasure? Well, let me tell you, a whiff of shattered bottle is intoxication to the nose.

Blessed be thy nose, still doing its part. Without it the tongue was a lump of dull flesh. I scratched my head trying to discern what I was sniffing, an olfactory soup: plum pudding, dried figs, gasoline, lentils, and a hair of vanilla extract. The blend seemed lethal. I couldn't place the whereabouts of the spilled wine though I was sure it was a French Cabernet. Maybe it was a Chinon; it's happened to me before, worse still a Californian novelty. The frightening thought lingered, I had to nail down the right continent.

Sad as it is to say, many of the frequenters went with the sole purpose of getting sloshed, beggars' happy hour. You could loop the city in search of tastings, most of which gave you at least four, sometimes five samples per table.

So I swished my white, detecting lime peel, quince marmalade and glazed pecans. The pourer revealed the label, Greco di Tufo, before I had the chance to make a guess. I bit into the lip of my waxy cup when somebody tugged my shirt.

"Tagalong, aren't you," Luz said with a quizzical grin.

"What are you doing in my hangout?" I asked, wiping dribble from my chin.

"This is my hobby, too, you know?" Luz asserted.

"But I didn't know you went to these rinky dinks."

"Where else can you get good samples for free?" Luz said, sniffing the unknown Chilean. "Botrytis has plonk, Corked has cooked goods. They're even hoarding Fat Bastard by the gallon and now its Italian counterpart Il Bastardo and some Mouton Cadet spinoff."

"Ugh, and everything they pour tastes like buttered popcorn, even their Nouveau," I added.

Luz's fingers gently spread from the bottom to the top of her cup as though she were cradling an Easter egg. A nostalgic mist gleamed in her eyes.

"You know, I cut my teeth on Bordeaux right where you're standing," she said.

"So did I, mine was a Ducru –"

"Beaucaillou," Luz chimed in, "You lucky bastard."

I shrugged.

"Well, excuse me mine didn't have that kind of pedigree but it was, what I would consider an unsung hero – Greysac," she reported.

"Sure that's a good one."

"I got hooked."

We both bobbed toward the spit bucket, slightly bumping heads. Ouch, a nice kind of pain. We shared discolored grins, her teeth still a tad brighter and I got that nutty excited feeling that I wanted to jump through my skin, but instead I pinched the palm of my hand. There was a rush of things I wanted to say, but was afraid of rambling. It had only been a couple of weeks since I'd seen her, she hadn't been to the arena and I was dying to know how she was keeping herself occupied. We'd crossed into the neighborhood of conversational intimacy, a long way since stuffed animal days, I needed to grab a hold of her, that if she walked away it might be the last time I saw her. This single effect she had over me made me want her so much, yet I was terrified because any time I developed feelings for somebody I threw myself at them, poured my personal life onto their lap. I scared women away. I was tired of bullshit games, hard to get, but if I didn't show a bit of nerve she was going to walk.

"I never thought I'd see you again," I said.

"Makes two of us," she replied.

"What are you kidding? I figured I was a goner when I went on and on with all that Wittgenstein nonsense. Next time, I swear, I'll keep it in my back pocket."

"I must admit," Luz said, adjusting her leather bag's strap on her shoulder, "I never heard a Desmond Morris or Pliny the Younger knock-knock joke before."

"Many times I get blotted out whenever I slip into a shower of philosophical filibustering. Has that ever happened to you when people just tune you out? You can see by their faces that they're on a completely different page and you can't seem to keep yourself from blabbing. Well, I guess those days have long gone. I seldom go into detail anymore just because I hate getting those looks."

"Are you trying to tell me I'm special?" Luz said.

"I guess so."

"My dad always told me that I have a certain approachable quality."

In Vino Veritas

For the next few weeks, we spent Sundays in Central Park sipping wine from Dixie cups. It was our only chance to unwind from an otherwise grueling week. Luz seldom spoke to me while I was training for my upcoming thumb-wrestling bouts. That afternoon however, we parked ourselves on the browning lawn across Turtle Pond, sandals and sneakers off, and joked for hours. The sun's rays still packed a punch though it was the middle of Fall. We were a few drips from polishing off the second bottle, the Amarone. The less desirable Chianti lay on its belly hidden underneath a plastic supermarket bag. Luz wasn't fond of the Chianti she had brought and I felt badly about making such an emphatic stink, that it lacked backbone. Luz, in her heather turtleneck sweater, propped herself on her elbows and dipped her head back to catch the blood orange sun swooping behind the treetops. The San Remo Towers rose high above the pumpkin-colored trees as if guarding the western side of the city. Her mouth wrapped into a bow as she swallowed the last of the Amarone while I swirled mine staining the innards of my cup.

"This is a slice of heaven," she said.

"Chocolate mousse," I countered.

"It fills your whole mouth. You'll think I'm crazy but it tastes a bit like mole."

"I can see that. Ever had a recioto? Poor man's Amarone."

"No."

"Personally, I prefer a good Valpolicella. Very quaffable."

"Give me Gigondas, anything from the Rhone."

"You're such a Francophile."

"Then why did I bring Italian?"

We tapped cups and swigged.

"This is the life, sipping, snacking, so European," Luz said.

"Senior year, when I returned from Italy," I said, curling into an upright position, "I couldn't get used to the culture shock."

"How long were you away?"

"Winter intercession."

"Five weeks?"

"Something like that."

"Culture shock, give me a break."

"It was. Like getting off a carousal and everything swinging by too fast. I couldn't keep up."

"You know what your trouble is? You haven't taken a defining step."

"Maybe so."

"You need to uproot yourself. You're much stronger than you give yourself credit for. You've sold stuffed animals in the street."

I thought of walking cobblestoned streets without being bothered by people who knew me from my trick-or-treating days.

"Now, I'm afraid to mention this," Luz said with more heft to her voice. "I really think you ought –"

"Tell me."

"Forget your little five-week excursions. You come back to your cozy little bed and your mommy's home cooking, that's not going to cut it."

"Go ahead say it?"

"You need to move out. Get your own place. Pay the gas and electric bills. Then you'll feel grown up."

"Picasso said the trouble with most of us is just that, we grow up."

"You're not Picasso."

"Maybe so, but I have this funny feeling that if I do grow up it's going to be for good. I might lose my good-natured side."

"That's the chance you need to take."

Luz shifted to her right side and plucked the grass by her legs.

"Look, if it makes you feel any better," Luz said, "I'll help you find a place."

"I can do it on my own."

"As long as you make the effort; you can't just move back in with mommy if there's no hot water."

"You don't think I can do it, do you?"

"Of course I do, but you need to make it happen. You can't give up halfway through it the way you did with your thesis."

"What was I supposed to do? That numbskull professor, my sponsor, scanned my abstract then squiggled two sentences rejecting it – he didn't even turn the page."

"I just don't get it."

"It didn't make sense to me either."

"No, I mean you were so close to finishing it."

"I changed topics, formed a new hypothesis, collated more data, the whole nine yards. I returned eight months later, for more punishment. The appointment was for three o'clock, but he made me wait until four forty-five to complete his undergrad advisory nonsense. You'd think he'd prioritize. When he finally calls me in, he fusses with his stupid glasses, cleaning the lens and I hand over my folder. This time he reads it for twenty minutes, clears his throat a million times. I play good Samaritan and fetch him a cup of water. He spills it on my God damn thesis."

"No."

"Oh, yes. Then he chews on his pencil eraser and asks me if I know the underlying polemical driving my thesis. I tell him it boils down to repairing others misfired utterances, jargon confusion, and other stuff. He stares at me as if I'm a midget trying to slam dunk. Then he tells me focus, cut all my adjectives, highlight the three-syllable words, and only leave three sentences in a paragraph."

"And then what?"

"Oh, I was done. I hated my topic."

"But you love anthropology."

"Sure."

"So why didn't you pick something you loved?"

"What and go to Lake Turkana, Tanzania and dig up bones? What was I going to add to the fossil record?"

"What were you planning on doing with your thesis of misfired utterances?"

"Nothing. Nobody cares about it anyway."

"You're a sadist, a martyr."

"That's Catholic School."

Luz's big brown eyes were glazed. I got the funny feeling the way she parted her lips and how the crinkles by her cheeks broadened that she was on the brink of telling me something more. She grabbed for her cup and jiggled whatever was left then gulped.

"You'd make a great professor. What doesn't make sense to me is why you'd invest all that time if you weren't even interested in your topic."

"Sometimes you need to do things you don't want to do."

"By the same logic you should move out."

Apartment Hunting

After that, Luz took me apartment hunting. We checked for places advertised in throwaway newspapers. She also suggested scouring the pinup boards at local colleges, where I could find something in my price range, dirt cheap. The first place we saw was an oversized shoebox that stank of mothballs. The second was a one-bedroom-job, clearly a studio transformed by way of greed and a couple of sheetrock planks, into a one bedroom. The broker led me by the hand to show me the closet. "You could store a refrigerator in there," she told us. There was hardly anywhere else it could fit. The bedroom was almost big enough to fit an inflatable mattress and maybe a stack of magazines.

"How about a signal?" Luz said, between 7th and 8th Avenue. "I'll click my heels if we should split."

"I love it, a bit of irony on there's no place like home."

"Whatever, is that too subtle?"

"No, it's fine."

"And if I think you should give it a chance, I'll fold my arms."

"You got it."

Without Luz, I don't think I would have made it to the third place, a real dingy hole-in-the-wall, what I think they call a railroad apartment. This time we'd removed the broker from the equation, but the tenant was a bit strange. He made us take our shoes off before entering the apartment. Toward the kitchen, there was a dusting of kitty litter pebbles. This I learned the hard way, having to pick them off the bottoms of my socks.

He excused himself right away, ducked into his bedroom and left us to stare at his teakettle boiling on his gas stove. Why somebody would offer to show their apartment and then keep you waiting while they poked around in the other room was beyond me. After a few minutes, I was really getting claustrophobic since the layout of the apartment almost, but didn't quite, allow for two grown beings to walk alongside each other. The walls didn't come crashing in on us. When the whistle tooted and the guy returned lifting the kettle on the stove I flubbed cues, thinking that Luz, clicking her heels, meant give it a chance. His bonky nature had me off guard plus I was worried Luz might think I was giving up too easily.

"Won't you stay for some tea," he offered.

"Sure," I said.

"We really can't stay, I have a dental appointment," Luz said.

"No problem, I can take a look. I'm semi-retired now, but I can't seem to get teeth out of my head."

"Or kitty litter out of your toes," I added.

"Have a seat," he said. "I'll get my bag."

Luz looked at me as if I was to blame. I snooped around to see if there was any sign of a cat, but there wasn't a single hair on the couch, nor on the chairs.

"So if I take the place I'd have to feed the cat, is that part of the deal?" I shouted.

The guy moped back into the room with a well-worn leather bag in his hand and a look as if he'd forgotten what he was supposed to do next. He fished through the bag until he pulled out his dental doodads. He slipped on a pair of Latex gloves then tipped Luz's chin, "Say ah," he said.

"Ahhhhh."

He stuck a pencil-sized light into her mouth and began waving it. Luz's cheeks quivered.

"Hmm, just as I thought," he said, pinching one of her molars.

He let go of her tooth and put his light back into his bag.

"Everything alright?" I said.

"Nothing changes. People with good teeth always go to the dentist. There's so many rotting teeth and gums out there you can't even imagine. It's so frustrating sometimes I just want to go back into practice."

"Can you do eleven hundred for the place?" I asked. "I'll feed the cat for you too."

"There must be some mistake I thought you were coming over for the trunk," he said.

"The advertisement said twelve hundred for the apartment."

"Hmm, well it never really crossed my mind, but sure, why not if you don't mind sleeping on the couch, eleven hundred it is."

That's where I drew the line. The guy had this goofy expression as if he'd just hit the jackpot. Then he went on about all the great little eateries in the hood, but we politely worked our way to the door and excused ourselves. Luz slipped back into her flip flops and I didn't even bother with my shoes taking them in hand and made for the stairs.

He pushed his fleshy face up against the banister spokes and shouted down.

"Wait," he said, "How will I get in touch with you?"

"I'll let you know, manana," I said.

Catch As Catch Can

With little fuss I loaded a few imperatives and whatever else fit into my backpack, a duffel bag, and a cardboard box. This was how I left home, presumably for good, and my mother kept dropping in extra teabags, crackers, pieces of fruit, and boxer shorts she'd bought for the occasion, thus prolonging the inevitable goodbye.

There was a knot in my throat. I wasn't going to miss my mother's lousy cooking. The meatloaf that tasted like shoe leather or all those dingbatty juice concoctions she pulped in her turbocharged blender. I knew this time I was making an irrevocable move unlike my false start, two years earlier, which turned out to be a month and half vacation with numerous trips back to bilk groceries.

No, I didn't take the retired dental kook's pad. I took Luz's word about a place she'd scouted on her own. She said it would be perfect for me so I gave it a go and it was only a fifteen-minute cross-town walk to work.

The first night dragged, I wouldn't conk out, spooked by the dripping kitchen faucet and the hollow drone of rattling pipes. It was an old walkup with rusty fire escapes plastered to the building's facade, a ramshackle Hell's Kitchen tenement brimming with character from the crackling brick to the Ethiopian restaurant down below, honeyed meat and charred bread wafting up, seeping through the open window. Wires jutted out of the wall socket and there was a swerve of spots on the kitchenette ceiling reminding me of the Little Dipper. The linoleum curled in what might have been considered dining room territory. For some strange reason I had a craving for carpet, never had a rug as a kid.

It had been such a long time since I had slept alone, with nobody in the other room. The last time was when I crashed in an ATM booth in Madrid the day before I made the connecting train to Pamplona to run with the bulls. I had passed out from heat exhaustion and had a dream that I was sucked into a Goya and everybody I turned to ask directions from was nothing but a lost soul wallowing in grief.

With nothing worthwhile on television I hung my head over the chessboard, scooping cold macaroni from the pot. My thumbs needed to take a breather and my brain needed a charge. To play a decent chess game against your self is the pinnacle of enlightenment. Outthink yourself. Are you siding with one side over the other, your alter ego against your gut instinct? I mauled black's army until white had a solid material advantage. When all seemed hopeless I rallied black's defense.

Fewer pieces sharpen the drive. Tactics are tangible, either you hang on or get annihilated. I find myself with a Pavlovian thirst to save the underdog. A quiet game of solo chess and yet I hear the howl of the arena. It's not the whirligig of buzzing fans, but the hope I might be gentle to my softer side. There was something precarious about my newfound thumb-wrestling popularity, that if I sneezed hard enough I might knock myself out of this alternate universe. Sometimes I passed myself in the mirror confused at what I saw. I saw me, but which me exactly was it.

The last few years, I have seen myself as an underdog. Rooting for the underdog, I ended up rooting for myself, that I might rise to greatness.

I considered stealing white's initiative and unleash black's counterattack. This became my mental masturbation. The warbling staccato of car alarms had me up anyway.

The third night there was a knock on the door. Not very loud, mind you, but it made me jump. I went to the peephole. It was Luz, holding two valises; a long herringbone coat fell over her shoulders like a cape. I rushed out to greet her like a puppy who hadn't seen its master in months and of course the door slammed behind us; I hugged her and we rolled on the floor. When I tried to open the door it was locked.

"Tell me you have your keys?" she said.

"Okay, I have them," I replied.

"That was a close one."

"They're inside by the kitchen sink."

From the outside of the tenement, I latched onto the butt end of the fire escapes. With a boost, I wormed my wiry frame to the fourth floor. Fortunately, the window was left ajar, otherwise I would've needed to crowbar my way in. I never got the impression Luz was that worried, while I hung there with dangling limbs, even when my slipper dropped off. Her poise was effortless, her round face demure. She leaned over the railing like a trapeze artist and tapped her open palm on the rusty metal with stolid brio capturing the beat of my heart.

That was how Luz moved in. Something to do with her old landlady, she didn't want to discuss it and I didn't mind; I was happy just to have her. None of those sob stories about the impending ho humdrum after you've moved in with somebody were going to shatter my dreams. We weren't really a couple anyway so none of those old wives' tales about fossilized freedom would apply.

I was thoroughly fascinated by her peculiarities, for instance the way she caught her reflection off things, even off the side of the toaster. She always stuck the toilet roll on so the paper rolled in a clockwise fashion, whereas I preferred to have it roll counterclockwise. Incidentally, she

74

kept the paper streaming down and I rolled it back whenever I had the chance.

She was a sometimes vegetarian. When it came to Mexican food she made the exception. There was this cheap Mexican eatery, Pico de Gallo, around the corner that made stellar tortas. We ate Pico's twice a week: once in person, once for takeout.

"Now this is Mexican," Luz said, biting into her puerco enchilada. She picked out the onions and slabbed them onto my plate. In return, I dumped the hot peppers onto her refried beans.

For a couple of months we were inseparable, she came home, dropped her bag on the doorknob and nosed into my doings. We shared bags, not bowls of chips because it was more intimate, our greasy fingers groping for salty goodness. A frisky grin here, some tickle tickle there. She hated pizza, but I loved it. We'd sit in a pizza joint, I snacked on a Sicilian and she'd pick at a scone and sip coffee.

I'm not sure who decided to do what, but we seemed to end up at different places. Sure there were heated discussions, Luz was fiery; she welcomed verbal jousts. Usually, I backed down. I guess I was a born diplomat or maybe an educated doormat.

A mid September Blackout caused our fray. I'd taken a mental health day from thumb-wrestling. I'd been napping and awoke close to four o'clock. After a few failed attempts to turn the T.V on I realized there was a power outage. I didn't know where the fuse box was and if I did I wasn't sure what to do with it. The fridge was empty except for soy packets, a mangled tortilla half, and a topless jar of peanut butter. I stuck my head under the kitchen faucet and drank three gulps then decided to get some fresh air and maybe a can of Mountain Dew.

The streets were jammed with people. I figured there might be a celebrity sighting or somebody prepping to jump from a ledge.

"What going on?" I asked some guy.

"Man, it's a Blackout."

I'd been too young for the last big one back in the late seventies, what was a major doozy for the city: looting, the Bronx burning. The last I recalled a Brownout hit a couple of years ago. Astoria suffered most from these nasty electrical hiccups. The irony being Con Ed stood smack in their hood.

This Blackout had a pleasant vibe, an urban Carnival. By evening, delis handed out ice-cream sandwiches, Bomb Pops, and cold cut slabs. The beer and soda was warm, but heck it was free.

No sign of Luz. Every so often I checked the apartment, but no dice. Finally, I got excited by nine o'clock when I poked in and heard the water running in the kitchen. The room shined obsidian. Nope she wasn't in the bathroom. Then I went into her bedroom. For a second, I thought she might be lying down. The blanket folded in a lump to the side of the bed. My elbow twitched. I felt my pulse racing. When I smoothed the blanket across the empty bed a hollow note filled my soul. A door slammed on the floor below. The creaks and groans of the old building tailed me onto the fire escapes and waited out there watching the world sweep by fretting for Luz.

Past midnight she returned with her camera and tripod. She flopped on the couch and I banged my head rushing to climb back into the apartment. Enough of my quibbles. I tugged off her shoes and socks.

"What a day," she said.

"I was worried about you," I said, forcing a grin.

"It was wild I tell you, but I got awesome footage."

"Really."

"I'm making headway on my project."

"The Luddites?"

"And counting. Leave it to a crisis. This one guy bragged that he carried a flashlight everywhere, but didn't own a calculator or a landline."

I wanted to see her footage. I wanted us to stay up all night and talk now that everything in the world hummed. Luz was bushed though, passed out. I carried her to her bed and put her to sleep.

Things changed from that day. Not only was I seeing less of her, too wrapped up on her documentary, she hardly bothered visiting the arena and was seldom around the apartment. She did leave behind matchboxes, all from fancier digs than our torta shack.

Often, I ate chuletas asadas alone, but ordered chilaquelas for Luz hoping she'd drop in for dinner. Sometimes she brown-bagged the leftovers for her lunch.

She stayed out late at night and though I was insanely curious to know where she'd been, I never pried. I assumed my spot, waiting by the window to see her walk down the block, the lights off. When I heard her creaking up the stairs I slumped on the couch and pretended to be asleep so she wouldn't think I'd waited up for her.

These silly things sculpted me into a man. Without her, you could say I'd still be back at home with the folks, waking up with a pile of laundry on my belly and a postcard with a list of chores to do around the house.

I bought a goldfish bowl and lumped the matchbooks together, a mountain of evidence.

"I think we need to start smoking," I said one day.

Luz didn't crack a smile. Sometimes I had the feeling she only wanted to be roommates. It pained me to see her walk by as if I was air. It reached a point that I dared myself to slip underneath her covers in the middle of the night. Going from my pullout couch and into her bedroom was quite a stretch in the ebony stillness. As soon as I neared the critical threshold, her doorway, I froze.

She slept in a ball, her legs splayed sharply to the side, forming a right triangle. One night after I drank a whole bottle of an Australian cheapie, I ventured into her room while she snuggled with her comforter. I lost the nerve as she flopped over, catching me by surprise, with my hand under her ear. She was startled, so I pretended that I'd seen a mouse scurry into her room, which was why I went in. This didn't pan out to be such a good alibi as she hopped out of bed frenetically pursuing the broom. She swatted under the bed and the radiator.

She stopped by the arena a few days later. She didn't bother waving hello or anything, but tended to her business with Mungo while I was scrimmaging with one of my practice partners. Mungo wore pouches under his eyes and his shoulders drooped. He didn't have that brooding presence he usually brought into a room. Luz kept her arms tight to her chest, shaking her head every so often. Mungo reached for her hand, but she brushed him off.

So maybe I acted a bit jealous with Luz and it wasn't fair to her because she wasn't leading me on, but I had to know what brought her to that rotten thumb-wrestling arena in the first place and more importantly what was the deal with her and Mungo. I waited until our Sunday picnic before saying anything.

We perched on the rocks overlooking Wollman Rink and predicted which skater would take the next spill. By dessert, I finally broached the subject and Luz gave me the kind of look as if I'd been imagining things.

"I'm not buying it for one second," I said to Luz, craning my neck to get a nibble of her cupcake.

"Think what you want, it's really none of your business anyway," she said pulling her cupcake away from me. Some of the chocolate sprinkles spilled onto my shirt.

"I'm just looking out for your best interest," I said. "He's an animal. You don't really know what he's capable of."

She got up and yanked the blanket from underneath me.

"Luz, wait a second."

"If you must know, he's my father."

"What? No way. You don't even look alike!"

"It's a long and complicated story," she said, folding the blanket end over end into a ball.

"I highly doubt it. People always say that when it's really very simple and they don't feel like telling too much. Either he is or he isn't."

77

"Forget about it," she said, tripping over the rocky patch that had a giant gash splitting down the middle, a leftover from the last Ice Age. She smirked a little when she gained her balance, perhaps remembering what I'd told her about it the last time we came to the park.

"You brought it up," I said, trying to get a hold of some of the junk: the basket or the blanket from her hands.

Luz marched down. I kept pace and watched the muscles tighten in her neck like she was rock-climbing.

"Hey, check that one there. Doesn't it remind you of Magilla Gorilla?" I said looking skyward. I raised my brows to encourage Luz to do the same.

"Not really," she said.

I shaded my forehead, "You know my affinity for apes. I see them everywhere."

I pointed to the cloud puffing by, but she shook her head.

"Didn't he play the ukulele?" I said.

"Most people get the wrong idea about him," Luz said.

"But he's soft on the inside like a Magilla Gorilla," I said.

"What are you talking about?"

"You know."

"Look, if you really want to know, he's my adopted father."

"No reason to get sore about it. I take back what I said earlier."

"You just don't get it."

"How am I supposed to if you never clue me in?"

She looked at me with sad brown eyes. More than anything, I wanted to get her meaning without her having to spell it out, to understand what was gripping her, and I felt she wanted that too, but I couldn't read her, not then.

"Let's call a truce for now," I said.

She fished around her pockets for a piece of gum. When she found some she broke off half with her teeth and offered me the bigger piece.

Mungo's Motto

Mungo's sneeze sounded like an Uzi as the rubber ball whizzed by my sneakers. I don't know how I let him talk me into a game of handball, but he could hustle for somebody his size and shape. He chewed a big wad of gum that a mere mortal would probably choke on while dashing back and forth.

"You know how I made it, Benny?" he said, wiping his face off on his T-shirt.

"Actually, I haven't a clue."

He smashed the next shot zipping egg-like toward my head and I slapped it back high off the wall, but somehow Mungo grabbed air and deflected my shot, sending it into the corner where I was barely able to get my fingers on the ball. My whole left hand went numb so I was pretty much handicapped since my right was nothing but deadweight. With a last stabbing effort I blooped the ball back, right-handed, and it dribbled back into Mungo's crushing zone and he let loose a roundhouse whap rifling the ball past me.

"You probably think I earned my stripes breaking legs, don't you? A punk kid, with a chip on his shoulder smashing parking meters with a baseball bat so that he could live like a king in the arcades."

"That really never crossed my mind."

"Well, I'm sorry to disappoint you but none of it is true. Truth is, I've always been a gambler. No surprise there. It all goes back to my bocce days. I was some player in my teens. Went to the park every day so the old timers could show me the ropes. In return, I took their lunch orders. They always bought me a sandwich too, Cokes, Eskimo pies whatever I wanted.

"There's a certain art to bocce and even though it's kind of like lawn bowling, the two are mutually exclusive entities. You follow. For one, we play on clay while lawn bowling, like the name implies, is played on grass. And we have a court, fitted with stone sides that the ball caroms off. Ever played a game?"

"Can't say that I have."

"Next time it's bocce."

"Whatever you say."

"You should see the old park. It's beautiful, down in the old neighborhood, Bensonhurst. Let me tell you, you can't find better brazgiole. Mama mia, their sausage and peppers are out of this world."

"So let me get this straight, you want me to add bocce to our repertoire."

"What are you, a jooch?"

"No, ah, just figured that your little story was part of the plan."

"Keep the figuring to me. What's the matter with you? Bocce is sacred."

"I didn't mean any disrespect."

"You need a good kick in the pants every once in awhile."

The thought struck me that I'd get a solid boot in the pants, maybe even a bat across the skull if he know about Luz's living situation. Somehow the infinite Technicolor bubble looping from his lips made him seem less of a monster. Luz was the compassionate part of the equation.

"Little by little I built my bocce skills till I was better than everybody in the park. But the egos of some of those galoots couldn't match my skill or my ability to keep everything on ice. I was so cool that some of the old timers wanted to test my luck with poker. No dice for me, I loved the outdoors. It was bocce or bust. Then along came handball, badminton, horseshoes. Yes sir, I was an ace. What, you can't imagine me skinnier than I am now?"

"No, not at all," I said. "I mean, of course I can. You probably were a beanpole back then."

"Damn straight. I would've whipped your butt even worse if it weren't for my knees. When I was younger I dove on the cement for those corner shots."

He rolled up his pants revealing a scattering of crescent shaped scars, two of them bifurcated into what appeared to be a broken cross.

"So you're probably wondering how did I learn to hustle? Well, it's simple. I was born to hustle. I never was the greatest player, but I knew whenever I was up against a hotshot I made sure the deck was stacked in my favor. I'm telling you this because I still think you're a good kid and I think we can make beautiful music together. But for Chrissake, stop trying to be a world beater, you look constipated when you're deep in your matches. We all know you're freaking gifted, but just relax and enjoy yourself a little more."

"I'm gifted, seriously?"

"So I need to ask for a little favor."

"Sure, what do you need me to do?"

"We've been raking it in for a while. Real good, can't complain. But you're becoming a bit of a favorite. And being as such, we've got to throw a lot of good money your way just to keep it reeling in and to be quite honest, I'm getting tired of the smaller fries. Get my drift?"

"Sort of."

"Well, it's going to be like this, I need you to take a dive, for your next bout. That way I'll be able to clean up. You with me?"

"I guess so; I was just hoping to keep my streak alive a bit longer, what with the chance to break Lefty Lawson's record."

"The hell with that. What do you think I'm running here, a charity? I don't give two shits whether or not you have some stupid record. Maybe you should do more grunt work."

"No, everything's cool. I was just wondering."

"Stop wondering."

"You just tell me which event and I'll be down for the count."

The Sacred Handoff

Despite Mungo's proclamation I went back to my workout, squeezing tennis balls, doorknobs, grapefruits. I never made so much fresh squeezed juice and with all that healthy crap I didn't want to get too out of whack with my proclivity for junk food so I indulged to find my sense of homeostasis. You hear horror stories where people go cold turkey, no smoking, no booze, all organic, they run exercise bikes until their legs fall off and they're in tip top shape and then they drop dead of a heart attack while checking their mail.

There were all kinds of ways to train. Crushing walnuts with your bare hands was supposed to be another good thing to do. Many of the challengers sparred with each other. They had their own circles, knew each other from here and there, they razzed each other and even played their own form of Russian roulette. One guy with a hammer in hand, the other numbskull kept his fingers fanned out on a table while the hammerer whacked between the numbskull's fingers. They hurried the pace. It was horrific when somebody smashed bone.

I stopped by my old stomping grounds since I missed seeing what antics my hairy friends were up to. It had been over a month. Up to the twenty-ninth floor. I had almost forgotten what a spectacular view there was from some of the offices, but not for the monkeys. Thelonious, in particular missed me; he gave me a high-five when I set foot into the firing range. Deep within his mellifluous eyes I could see a pain that I'd known all too well, the knot you get from absorbing too much while sharing too little. If Thelonious had a grasp of sign language I would have signed him to someplace better, out of his dart-slinging daze, but he had, much like me, mastered the art of getting by.

Though he was capable of producing so much more, music, emotions, he wasted away. He remained a cruel twist of design trapped by a system that stunted his growth. He hadn't a son to pass the baton or in this case the dart to, the way Jasper, Nietzsche and all the others had. What he had going for him despite his meager prospects was an impenetrable callowness that allowed him to bask in complacency.

Thelonious hooted, coaxing me to follow him to the other end of the room. His face was full of wonder, as though he saw beyond the opaqueness confining him to the dusty walls. The lights faded until we were shrouded in darkness. From the corner of my eye, I noticed Jasper inspecting me, the unwelcome traitor.

With the pugnacious baboon's head turned, my buddy dropped a celery stick in my hand. Jagged by the end it was quite apparent that it had been gnawed. Thelonious's favorite vegetable was more than a vegetable, it was his source of serenity, conducting the music that filled his being. He clasped my hand shut around the celery. This was his baton and he was handing it off to me, what exactly I was going to do with it I had no idea.

Idiot's Guide To Climbing The Umbilical Cord

There was of course more than just one fall. I'd made a pin, I'd take a fall. This back and forth went on and Mungo cleaned up. I went from a thumb-wrestler to a yoyo. As Mungo said, he wasn't running a charity, but I was beginning to lose fans or I should say they had become fair-weather. Sometimes they cheered for me and other times they booed me. I hit the bottle a bit more. I sulked at free tastings after my matches as a way to lick my wounds, but I spit out into the bucket as a force of habit.

Training was optional but I did some just to squash any rumors that I was a Fall Guy. I did as I was told throwing my matches because I needed to pay off my credit card debt and Mungo paid me double to get pinned. For years, I had been postponing the inevitable, but with prohibitive rates rising geometrically faster than my earnings I needed to take action. How could I have incurred so much debt you're wondering, especially since I'd been living with my folks for so many years? Well, to put it mildly for a number of years I spent like I had six months left to live and bandied about the idea of declaring personal bankruptcy and start over with a clean slate. There was a method to my madness. Luz was the gadfly behind me. She put her foot down when I'd mentioned it offhandedly. It didn't sit well with her and I needed, of course, for things to sit well with her. I couldn't tell her that I'd been getting further behind on my bills because, dumb ass me, I didn't have all my mail forwarded to our apartment so I told Luz I had a system for paying off my credit cards, at the bank.

She didn't buy it. She said on an unconscious level I kept some mail going to my parents to have a safety net in case things didn't work out on my own.

Six days a week I was a slave. You know the fleshy pouch that connects your thumb to the rest of your hand, well, it went numb. In fact, it became hard so I put it to good use, hammering things around the apartment with it. There was no reason to let an advantage like that slip by. The closest feeling I could compare it to was when, during my wasted pubescent years, I'd been on a mission to gobble up video game winner circle patches. Little did I know, back then, that all the fumbling with joysticks would one day come in handy. Actually, my whole right hand was numb. This was worse than when I'd lost my nail, the one that snapped off because I got smashed with a baseball during a chilly spring batting practice.

I'd learned that my mom had paid those bills I was worrying that I'd misplaced. I was pretty steamed about it. This was just another strike against me and showed my incapability of taking care of myself.

"So what was I supposed to do, let your credit rating go to hell in a hand basket?" Mom told me over the phone.

"No, but you could've let me know what you were up to," I said.

"I'm damned if I do, damned if I don't. So tell me, this new roommate of yours, does he have to pick up after you?"

"Good gravy."

"I'm just asking because it's hard to find somebody trustworthy to live with and from what you told me he sounds like a nice fellow. But just be careful. Don't leave anything with your social security lying around."

"He's great. Just fantastic."

"I picked up the little shell pasta you like and those sour dough pretzels. I'm not giving them to you until you come over."

"Bribery, is it?"

"You have to pick up your mail too."

"Ugh. That's it. I can't go on like this."

"Oh, don't be so overdramatic. Your father wants to show you something too when you stopover."

"What?"

"He mounted something of yours, one of your baseball awards. Shhh. Don't let him know I told you."

"I won't."

"If you come by tomorrow I'll make some cutlets. Would you rather have string beans or broccoli?"

"String beans. This nut I live with is always leaving raw broccoli around and forcing me to eat it."

"I'll cook ours."

"Still, I've had enough of it."

"I have to meet him. You should bring him over sometime. Not tomorrow, I mean I won't have enough to go around, but you can bring him over next week. Come to think of it the week after would be better. Your father has his KKK meetings to go to. He'd like to meet your friend as well."

For the record I should mention that my dad wasn't a white-hooded piece of trash. That was my mom's attempt at humor. She always called his Knights of Columbus the KKK for some reason.

Of course I hadn't told them I was living with a woman. God forbid my mom knew I was shacking up with Luz, she'd never let up on me. She'd bug me at least ten times a day, as if she didn't do that already, but the questions would be more intrusive, she'd rifle them off till she got answers.

She wanted to see me once and for all settled down, provided we were all living under the same roof. Now, she hadn't met Luz or even heard me mention her name, not just yet. My mom gloated to her friends how close she was with me. The thing was she really didn't know a heck of a lot about my personal life. Only the scraps I wanted to toss her.

She got her hopes up too high, higher than I did mine and neither of us, how can I delicately put this, were pole-vaulters, so we inevitably set ourselves up, time and again, for disappointment. There was no reason to disappoint both of us. Then there was that 'my only son' factor. She couldn't lose me to just any skirt. That special someone had to be worthy. I used to think that nobody would be good enough, according to her, but over time I'd learned she only wanted me to be happy and the sad part was Luz had that special something my mother would find to be the perfect match for me. It was sad in two ways, first because I couldn't have her and secondly, were my mom to find out I was living with Luz I'd be forever ridiculed for letting her go.

A Spoonful of Indiscretion

Five in the morning and the numerals flashed on the alarm clock. I was groggy and heard noise coming from the kitchen. I got up to see if Murphy had returned.

Luz hated that I named our mouse. She thought I made a major faux pas, that by christening him with such a foolish name I had extended a permanent invitation to him. Baloney, he came and went as he pleased anyway. That and I didn't see the harm in treating him like a drop-in neighbor. Luz was just mad she hadn't been able to crush his brains over the floor the other night swinging and whiffing many times with the broom. Well, in any event it was nice to know she dropped in now and then. From the matchbox she left on the counter I could see she had been to the hot new Cuban place, Manteca. Apparently, she'd also broken her heel, only the shoe was visible at the top of the garbage bag. She left me some of whatever dessert it was she had, in a plastic container, but unfortunately our friend got to it first.

I was too lazy to futz with the jiggly shower nozzle so instead I peeled off my underwear and fetched the cleanest pair underneath the heap of spurned garments destined for laundry detail. Swabbed some roll-on deodorant under the old armpits and voila, I was a new man. There wasn't any reason to shave just yet and I let the stubble carry on for another day. I had a steadfast belief in never shaving more than twice in a single week.

There were no matches scheduled and it was raining so I had no intention of setting foot outside. When I got that loafing feeling I indulged. I nuked a leftover mollete, my favorite snack in the universe. The cheese bubbled with brio. Washed it down with tap water then dug around the cabinet above the Fischer-Price-looking stove, which we hardly ever used, except for boiling water for tea and pasta.

The only appetizing thing in the whole cabinet were graham crackers, but when I pulled down the box it turned out to be a bunch of oatmeal packets and a few handfuls of sunflower seeds wrapped in two separate sandwich baggies. I tore them open and gobbled them down.

Nothing was on the tube but crummy B movies, homemade work-out videos and game shows. The newspaper couldn't hold my interest and there weren't enough plates piled in the sink to entice me into doing any washing. I had no intention of putting the pullout back into its couch position as always, so I loafed a bit on my makeshift bed. With the apartment all to myself I found it easy to slip into Luz's room for a stuffed animal or a pair of her panties, anything really to cuddle with. My body trembling with shiftless willpower I was so close to consigning my urges over to my former lap-dancing queen Bubbles, but frankly I hadn't the faintest idea where her number was, plus she'd be passed out so early in the morning.

Suffice it to say a randy-looking doll came to my aid, still packaged, what presumably had been earmarked as a present for Luz's niece. Thick lustrous lips protruding from supple, sultry skin and curvaceous to say the least, the kind of doll that seemed better suited for pole-dancing. The packaging too was a bit provocative, shocking pink. Slung up inside the box the doll begged to pop out from behind its peep booth packaging. Nothing akin to the frumpy Strawberry Shortcakes and Holly Hobbies I remembered girls playing with when I was a kid. This plastic sex kitten with a scrumptious tumble of hair spilling over her shoulders, her eyes tattooed with a come hither expression lured me onto my knees.

I ran my thumbnail through the top of the box and sheered the cardboard edge. I slid out the doll sniffing the delicious scent of vulcanized plastic coated with flammable paint. My stomach gurgled. I messed with the hair a bit and arched its back so that the breasts were prominent. I puckered up and blew kisses and began to pleasure myself.

As I was getting all worked up, a scratching from the keyhole startled me. Sweat sprouted below my brows. Clutching the side of the couch, I swerved into an upright position while squashing the pillow with my elbow. My legs flopped over the back of the couch, but the door was open before I could make it over the other end.

A splash of horror washed across Luz's face. She took stock of my manhood and I was certain she was ready to bounce me out on my most sensitive appendage when she noticed her doll was lying on the edge of the pullout.

"What on earth?" Luz said, quickly slamming the door behind.

It was humiliating. Not only wasn't I getting it on with her, but she saw me in the act with her doll. The fire escapes were a few strides away but my pants cuffed my ankles and as I struggled to shimmy them up I stumbled nearly knocking out my tooth. Luz chased me.

We floundered by the couch. Spools of torridness swirling within her eyes, she wanted to kill me, I thought. The doll just lay there on the bed; sweat glistening on the back of my neck. I grew molten hot.

So maybe she wasn't like most women and maybe by luck of some libidinous cosmographer my calling had been set. Before I knew any better the two of us were entwined. We couldn't peel each other's clothes off fast enough. Her bra and panties perched atop our tangled pants.

She climbed on top of me and began riding me, savagely wriggling her hips. She tossed her head back, leaving her hand by her neck. I took her finger and began sucking on it. It tasted sweet like berry lotion. She then took me by the waist and switched positions so that she lay flat on her back, her nipples perked up, like pencil erasers. I lay atop her, pulsating against her belly and she throttled beneath my twisting pelvis. She dug her nails into my chest and made twin crescent moons.

We cooled off for a little bit, both of us lying on our backs, only to spoil things with meek and muddled words.

"You shouldn't leave such slutty dolls lying around," I said, half-joking, my eyes vacantly tracing the grease-spotted Little Dipper on the ceiling nearest the kitchenette.

"Like it's her fault. What if I tell my niece that you were playing with your Pikachu over her doll?"

We burst into laughter, as if we were schoolgirls sharing secrets about each other's first sexual encounters. Then we went at it again. By the end of our merrymaking I'd smashed my knee three times: into the coffee table, the metal crook of the pullout couch and once, purely accidentally, into Luz's chin. There were plenty of baby kisses to make her booboo feel better after that. We tossed and tugged, groped and groaned for hours. We rolled around like Greco Roman wrestlers.

After we spent ourselves we canoodled on the scuffed wooden floor still gazing into each other's eyes, the two overgrown fetuses that we were coiled around each other. The pungent smell of sweat and sex in the air was brutally intoxicating. Nay sayers can talk until they're blue in the face, but only the two of us would know just how sensual it was having a splinter tweezed out of the butt with somebody's teeth.

"I feel like some fresh pineapple," Luz said, arms tucked under her head.

"They're not really in season," I said.

"I'm just so thirsty, but I want something juicy. You know what I mean?"

"I think so."

"When I was kid my mom used to make the best juices. Guavas, mangoes, tamarind. I used to love chewing on the skins when she peeled them. But there were so many of us, my sister and my two brothers. And my cousins practically lived in our place. So my mother watered down our juice. It bothered me and I complained about it, but we were poor and I didn't want my papa to feel ashamed, that we didn't have enough juice. Manuela, my sister, used to tattle on me right there in front of everybody and I'd feel like a snake."

I slid toward the edge of the bed and reached onto the floor for my pants.

"What are you doing?" Luz said.

"I'm going to find you a big, juicy pineapple."

"Let's have water instead."

She didn't have to say it, but I could see it in her eyes. She wanted me to stay by her side and hold her. I didn't even bother with the water. We held each other for a while. Sometimes my eyes slid over her shoulders down her side to her hips, but I held her so close that I was limited in what I could see and I felt she was happy that way. My right arm went numb because I was leaning with all of my weight onto my elbow. There is no commandment for how long one must cuddle after having sex with a partner for the first time. I've always seemed to do the wrong thing, pull away too soon. Put my shirt back on, something. For some reason, I get cold after having sex and sometimes shiver. Not my legs just my arms and chest. The blanket curled beneath Luz's pale hip. I'm not sure if her tracing finger on my chest or my typical shivers were causing my goose bumps but I wasn't going to budge this time.

A Neuter Drip

The next day I spent alone at the zoo. I wasn't a regular or anything like that, but every so often I enjoyed keeping time with animals as you might have already guessed. Brig's foreboding held no weight. Of course I would come back to the zoo; it was my place of refuge. Since Luz was gone by the crack of dawn I took the day to sort things out. I was scared. There was no guarantee about anything and if I moped around the apartment I would only be haunted by her scent.

The snow monkeys stretched out as though bored with the whole day. Too many stupid kids throwing monkey faces at them I guess. They lobbed back peevish grimaces, without a clue nor a care in the world what their cousins were slinging at newspapers downtown.

I'd heard that in Tokyo hundreds of them could live one atop of the other as though a warehouse of stuffed animals. My bastardized image saddened me. One of the snow monkeys reminded me of Thelonious. He picked up a twig cocked it behind his ear and proceeded to hurl it my way. Wasn't quite the same as being handed a prized hunk of celery but the insinuation was too much for me so I found reprieve in the Penguin House.

It was always quiet there, mainly because it was too cold for most people, but I loved watching those tuxedo-garbed birds slice through the icy water. They shot through like torpedoes then hopped back onto the land, flapped the water off themselves then went back in for another dive. They were so much like those wind-up penguins I remembered as a kid that plodded up the sliding pond then swished down one right after the other.

I fixed on what appeared to be a couple teasing each other with their slanty snouts. All the fresh fish you could hope for and hours upon hours of lovemaking in a giant pool without fretting over pruning fingers. It could even be kinky, what with all the crowds swinging by to catch us in the act.

Somebody opened the door for just a moment and a flood of light poured in. The person didn't stay and when the door closed a narrow cone of light remained. When it evaporated an oblong darkness draped over me in the chilly room. I sunk into my seat thwarted by an inscrutable hollowness. I'm not sure if it was strictly the room's cold condensation finally hitting me, that is to say purely physiological or maybe a change in my mood affected me. I dwelled on a moment from youth when I was nine and at my Aunt Chloe's graduation ceremony.

Showers ruined the morning and my family had to wait it out. There wasn't any decent shelter, but a few trees. No tent, and the main building was practically across campus. I sulked on a scraggy, foldable wooden chair, waiting impatiently for the MC to wrap up ceremony after two unsuccessful attempts. The rain subsided, but a hermetic wetness soaked through my pants until my skin, bones and beneath, went numb and a neuter sensation had overcome me. I was wearing corduroys. Garbled thoughts filled my head and then it all blacked out leaving me with this vapid cloak of nothingness so that I couldn't even be sure that my body filled my clothes. By the time Aunt Chloe received her Master's degree in Sociology, there was a scattering of applause, and for the moment I felt fine. At least I thought I did. Every so often afterwards, I got the neuter feeling that I associate with wet corduroys spackled to my legs. When I hit puberty, that stupefying day hit me hard sometimes and I didn't feel like blood was rushing through my veins.

Shrouded within the nocturnal abyss of the Penguin House it struck me that I might never again taste Luz the way I had. She'd eke out of my life and remain a figment of my sensual past. I tried blotting this out, but a blinding luminescence spewed forth as though rocket dust spat from the mammoth tank.

When the door cracked open again that heckling sweep of light vanished and a family bumbled in pushing their stroller and piggybacked child up to the base of the glass.

Once again I had her unmistakable impression emblazoned in me, tooth marks too. I sunk back into the seat and spent the rest of the day wishing the two of us were penguins flying through the water. Penguins, after all, were one of the few animals, birds really, that mated for life. Then I recalled that was really only in captivity, but in the wild they only remained with each other for a year.

Birthday Bubba

Something phenomenal happened on Luz's birthday that indeed changed her life dramatically and thus put the kibosh on us recapitulating our jubilee.

She never even told me it was her birthday and I'm not so sure she would've had I not overheard her dishing with her friend Sumi on the phone, but that wasn't the half of it. I couldn't believe she met him, the great saxophone-playing, former president Bubba Carlson. Luz didn't invite me for drinks when she planned to show Sumi the picture. I tagged along anyway. Sumi was waiting by the bar, all the way at the end. The barbacks kept lifting the flappable counter to bring in more ice and remove plates.

"Why don't we grab a table?" I suggested.

I was ignored. Luz sat next to her friend and I stood behind them since the other seats were taken. When Luz pulled out the picture with Bubba's arm wrapped around her as if ready to tango I felt my stomach twist into a rubbery knot. She was gorgeous in her gown, hair woven up, the way all those actresses during the Oscars had, but there was nothing phony about her smile, it was natural. Her eyes wide open, glimmering.

I knew it wasn't any trick photography. Sumi slapped Luz on the thigh and Luz slapped her back harder. I waved a twenty dollar bill to flag down the barkeep.

"What's he like, I mean, is he tall?" I asked.

"What kind of stupid question is that, of course," Sumi replied as if she had too met him.

"He's so cute," Luz said. "And he has this charm that you cannot capture from television. No surprise really, but he was a pretty good dancer."

"No way. You danced with him?" Sumi said.

"Kind of."

"How did you meet? Did he saddle up to you and say hey, baby?"

Luz turned so I only had her back.

"You remember Carlos Fuentes, the one I told you about who was trying to get me a job with the Argentinean Consulate?"

"Yeah, I think so," Sumi said.

"He waved over at me and I tell you, I nearly flipped out when I saw who he was standing next to. I ran to the ladies room to check and see if I was looking up to snuff and when I hurried back Carlos gave me this silly look, but I mean, I had to make sure I was presentable, you can never tell if somebody is leveling with you and you never get a second chance to make a first impression.

"So I wasn't just going to go over to him and shake hands and be on my merry way. Every idiot does that and I wasn't just going to swoon over him."

"So what did you do?" I asked.

"I went up to him casually and said nice scarf. He was taken aback. I touched the napkin that was wrapped around his wine glass and he sort of chuckled. It was a bit surreal. And Carlos gave me this look, out of the corner of his eye, as if he should have had the honors.

"Can you believe it? Bubba Carlson, Mr. President, actually confessed to me that he had been taking a mambo class, but that he was too shy to strut his stuff. So I had him put down his drink and dance with me. He was so shocked and I think the people around us were floored. Who's this chica who thinks she's hot shit right?

"Well, we did a meringue because the song changed from salsa as we walked down to the dance floor. He put his hand on my hip and I led him around like I was his seeing-eye dog."

"Wasn't Helen, ya know, the First Lady jealous?" I asked.

"She wasn't even there. Like that would've stopped me. Get your mind out of the gutter," Luz said pointing at Sumi.

"What? I didn't say anything," I said, when Luz looked my way.

I was glad to be recognized again.

"I know what you both are thinking. It was just a harmless dance. We were actually interrupted by, I think it was a secret service man, but I had Bubba Carlson by my side for that instance and I can't deny it my heart was racing. I've always wanted everybody around me to look and say, Look at her. Wow, she's somebody."

I felt terrible for Luz because I thought so much of her. I'm sure that her date, whoever he was, and everybody around her was soaring too, vicariously living through her, at least I would have been because when she came back to me I could say that's my girl, isn't she special.

It just irked me she thought that meeting the former president gave her validation. With softened hands I cradled the picture of her and Bubba Boy, hoping she stayed my friend a bit longer.

Dog Day Afternoon

Since she'd stopped coming by the arena, I had to see how she was spending her days. I'd grown tired of imagining what she did, night after night, based meekly on her souvenir matchbooks. The goldfish bowl three quarters full. For quite some time I wanted to trail Luz to see how she spent her days, but I respected her space. I'd prepared myself for the worst, that she was keeping time with a dashingly handsome man, whereupon coming face to face with him could only lead to a pitying sigh from her, that I had hit so low as to tirelessly follow her around town, a belabored puppy.

I went to the coffee shop where Luz was meeting Sumi. Luz was hungry so she devoured two gargantuan muffins, no coffee or tea for her until she had inhaled the two muffins. Sumi stirred her cappuccino, she took deep whiffs of it but I'm not even sure she took a sip. She was dangerously thin and there were, according to her, way too many calories in a single cup of cappuccino, so she sniffed at it.

You could tell it ate her up watching Luz decimate her food, without a care in the world if she gained pounds as opposed to the ounces Sumi fretted over. I indulged in the opportunity to soak Luz in from the other side of the room, using the paper for cover. The café was pretty crowded anyway, but I was careful to order a tea, stealing glimpses here and there the way I sometimes did when I was out with her, but knowing that she was unaware of my presence heightened my thrill.

It was early enough, before the lunch crowd came bustling in with their humongous appetites and their equally humongous attitudes. Sumi slumped her shoulders, pointing her chin with her phlegmatic air that made you just want to slap her across the face. She had a rent-controlled one-bedroom apartment in Chelsea, and had a tendency to drop this fact one too many times.

They didn't talk about anything special, in fact, if you didn't happen to know they were friends there were swatches of time that skittered by that made it seem as if they were total strangers forced into sharing a table. I think Sumi might have still been jealous Luz got to meet Bubba C.

They were paying the bill just as I was getting into an article on a long lost recording that had just been found in the basement of one of Lester Young's lover's homes. I was so absorbed that I had almost forgotten what I was doing in the café in the first place. After Sumi had intentionally missed pecking Luz on the cheek and had gone on her merry way, I tailed Luz who was now heading downtown.

Somewhere in the Teens and Third Avenue, Luz waited in a lobby. She was brought three dogs by two different owners. Then she picked up two more by south side Gramercy Park by the building with two knights in shining armor guarding its door. Two more across from the Italian Wine Merchants and grabbed a couple more along the way. It was like watching those sea monkeys I'd once gotten out of the back of a Spiderman comic come to life, multiplying before my very eyes.

She had nine dogs, on nine leashes wrapped around her delicate fingers and kept rewrapping the leashes so they wouldn't scurry too far ahead thus creating a kind of baseball mitt that looked something akin to what players from the olden days used to shag flies.

There was a husky, two Labradors, a Japanese Chin, an enormous poodle with a bouffant that could almost be taken for a graying Desi Arnez, a wooly Akita, whose bark imitated a vacuum cleaner. Another dog was pure mongrel. There was also one of those curious little fellows with the piggy tail and the squished face that I always forgot the name. Lastly, this anorexic-looking thing, the life sucked out of its cheeks and a face that could've been painted on, all joking aside was a dead ringer for Gene Simmons.

The furry caravan hauled her to Madison Square Park, to the dog corral and they behaved remarkably well, which impressed me, considering these New York City dogs were cooped up in apartments and really didn't get to roam around the way their country cousins did. We humans had a lot to learn from them, as far as getting along goes, but then again if I was treated to spas and massages and could run around, day after day, just sniffing butts anytime I felt the need, I too might jump through rings at the snap of a finger.

I lulled behind a tree while Luz let the dogs network in the corral. It surprised me seeing Luz with so many dogs. I didn't see her as the animal type. She mentioned she once had a cat, a stray that followed her home as a child. She had it for two weeks. Then one night, without leaving a note or a meow, she vanished into the night never to return.

Luz couldn't fall for an animal who had no true sense of home, despite the fact she was more cat than she could ever be dog. She didn't find it so amusing when I had said this and I was beginning to see why.

I wondered if this was her daily routine because the poodle seemed so fond of her, kneading his head up against her leg, his big wooly ears flopping about and a gnarled stick clenched between his teeth. He ducked down, pressing his chest into the dirt, with his big glassy eyes vying for Luz's attention. Gene Simmons flashed his tongue, but apparently didn't give much of a performance as Luz scratched the poodle's head instead. Then the poodle leapt up and raced the outer perimeter of the corral, flaunting the stick as if it were a baton. Apparently, this had become the animal trend.

After he had finished his lap a Golden Retriever, an outsider from the pack, picked up the Poodle's baton and trotted the same path as his Poodle pal.

I couldn't contain myself behind the tree any longer and sneezed, practically blowing my head off. People turned as if I set off a firecracker. Luz stared at me with daggers in her eyes.

Slowly approaching her I had the impression the dogs would form a wall. Some actually did clump together. Gene Simmons sneered as I approached.

I just happened to be in the neighborhood was not going to fly. She had that 'What the heck are you doing here?' kind of face. Then turned away and she ignored me. I knew then I had stumbled upon something sacred. Why should I have thought any less of her? But, that must have been what was going through her mind. I stripped her of her privacy. We were all just out earning a living – our dreams mattered most. I wished I had the goldfish bowl right then and there and her picture with Bubba Carlson so I could hold them up the trophies of her better life.

We didn't talk about that day, not once.

The Main Event

The big day finally arrived. I rolled out of bed late that morning so I rushed to the arena where Mungo sported a big smirk. His smugness had been getting to me so I said nothing. In his head, it had all been planned out. The odds were huge, in my favor. I'd been on a winning streak that Mungo had set up for me. I was steamed some of my fellow competitors considered me a hack for relishing my whirlwind of pre-meditated pins. I dared Gumless, Bruiser Bob, Simonizing Sowinski, Lenny "Knuckles" Piscapo, and Kamala the Ugandan Giant, to press me good. I taunted them with emasculating insults, I cursed their mothers. Gumless got disqualified trying to bite my hand. Lenny Knuckles had a heart attack. The emergency guys tore our grips apart. I was really scared and a little ashamed of myself for taking it all too serious, making the show a sham.

Mungo was probably going to kill me if I won the big match. We'd bonded over handball and the Opera so I guess I should have been able to tell him man to Mungo that I wanted to win. Instead, I had to make my point. I wasn't going to get a dime if I played it my way. On the other hand, Mungo was finally promising me a few grand to take this big fall.

When I saw Luz sitting in the second row with her legs crossed my hands got clammy. I wanted to believe she was there for me, but I couldn't discount the harsh reality that she was there for her dad. Either way, I didn't want to make a fool of myself, not in front of her. I remembered back to the first time she saw me compete when she came over and whispered good luck, her lips gently grazing my ear. She'd sent goose bumps down my back. I didn't disappoint that day and now I was getting a bit restless. My sweat grew more pungent, releasing all those hapless hormones. The buzz of the crowd bumped a notch and when Lulu squirted some water into my mouth it made my tongue feel fuzzy.

What did the money mean anyway? For me, it came down to pride. And truthfully I wanted a last chance to hear my name chanted. I was that tacky. Mungo was going to kill me after I won, but at least I wouldn't shame myself in front of Luz.

There were more categories than ever before. Many folks awaiting the super-hyped gimp grudge matchups the venerable paraplegic and the former triathlete who now made this freak show his bread and butter. There were still other bouts slated on the card. More categories meant more profits. Why they lumped us thumb-wrestlers into weight categories all of a sudden, was beyond me, but they did it all the same. It sort of dumbed down my whole underdog image, but what could you do about it.

Actually, the biggest attraction, strictly by the numbers, was between the twin tons, the Farmer brothers, who were moments away from squaring off. They had the narrowest spread since nobody could figure out which of the brothers had the advantage. Farmers turned couch potatoes turned tabloid tumblers. They had once cultivated cauliflower and oranges until they concocted a robotic device that quintupled their crop, patented the rights to their invention and sold it for beaucoup bucks.

This let them sag back and mold into lipid lugs. Some scout from Oshgosh followed them, promising to make them into Sumo stars, but by the wave of Mungo's magic wand they ended up here, posing for their big bout, their bloated guts forming a buffer, make that blubber zone.

Many saps had their money on Burt, the one with the larger, hairier mole on his neck, but it was Paul who had the eye of the tiger and maybe even the eye of newt in bloom. Call it what you want, but thumb-wrestling had become, much to my shock, more than just a dinky sport, surpassing bowling, jockeying poker for cable coverage. The commentator assured those that weren't in attendance that what they were watching on Pay–Per View would be what Wrestlemania Uno was decades ago.

The sneak attack, what many of us might recall from schoolyard days, was not in play after the qualifying rounds had ended. In the main draw it was thumb to thumb. Twisted arms coiling round each other for better positioning. These competitors had a lot in common with chess hustlers. The psych-out was prime and could make all the difference between a win and an unwelcome pin. The governing body for our tournament added an extra count; what ordinarily would be a pin to three became a pin to four. This cast a cloud of controversy over the entire event, but it made the competitors more fierce, squeezing tennis balls and crushing beer cans in the lobby to limber up before their impending rounds.

Since I was off to the finals in my respective weight class I too was under scrutiny, by the onlookers, the press, everybody it seemed, including Luz who uncrossed her legs, but now folded her arms tight to her chest.

Across from my circle was the penultimate match of the evening, Hector, the paraplegic, lined up at his post while Dune, the former tri-athlete, was carried in on a stretcher, having broken his other leg hours before his final round, trying to rescue a cat in a tree. He hadn't any intention of forfeiting so they carried him, four men hoisted him up on their shoulders, as though pallbearers escorting him to his funeral.

The fans – an eclectic clutch from three-piece suits to wife beaters in faded dungarees – waved foam thumbs; it seems that in addition to the ones stamped with Benny, there were some Hectors, Farmers, and Kokos, the last of which was going to be my opponent.

The lines to the snack stands were huge, snaking around the bend. You had three choices: corndogs on a stick, chilidogs in buns or fresh-chopped salads, courtesy of the Farmer brothers, who instead feasted on chilidogs [Burt] and a quintuple corndog for Paul minus the sticks, until that is, he needed his trainer to pick his teeth before the pre-fight photo session.

Dune, the former tri-athlete, was dumped into his seat and locked up with the paraplegic, their elbows anchored on the table, arching their arms so it almost seemed they were prepped for arm-wrestling. It was only the regular, non-gimp bouts that competitors stood, which occasionally made things more like real wrestling as was the case of my first few bouts. These gimp matches took the whole thumb-wrestling sport to a new level because with the table sandwiched between the competitors they had to make ample use of their thumb-thrusting skills. It wasn't as if they could slap on an arm-bar or any camel clutches or figure fours leg locks. Well, maybe the refs were clamping down on all that stuff in general, especially since we were getting the cable coverage. Mungo flaunted his spiffy pineapple shirt. The caster from Sports Buzz was doing a quick profile, Lulu, was of course in the background, pushing through the paraplegic's entourage to make sure things were kosher, and when he was satisfied he hung out by the front row. When Mungo was done with his interview he sat next to Lulu who was filling up on peanuts.

That same old lady from the last event was there again, this time with a cane, a blue bonnet and Elton John type sunglasses. She pumped her fist for the paraplegic, twisting her head with every move he made.

When the paraplegic had made the pin and sprang from his wheelchair, somebody from the audience shouted, "It's a miracle!" The arena went nuts, his cronies quickly pulling him out of there but not before some irate fan bashed a chair off the paraplegic's head.

Without any further ado, my match got under way. The crowd seemed foggier to me than usual. Took me a while to realize that was partly because of the smoke spewing from the machine they had set up by the bottom of the ring.

The announcement was distorted, what you might hear from your scuba instructor during an underwater lesson. The crowd cheered and somebody tossed a bunch of flowers in my general direction. One of them had nearly been plucked clean.

Koko was jumping around. I think he was under the mistaken impression we were going to duke it out for the finale. He may have been scrawny but he had a mean look about him; the kind of kid who skipped burning ants with a magnifying glass and went straight into squirrel hunting with a bow and arrow. He cracked his knuckles off his chin then curled into a ball stretching out hamstrings and his buttocks by hugging his knees to his chest. I'm not sure if we were prepping for the same event.

Unfortunately, I stepped on a gob of gum. Probably Mungo's discard, seeing that he was chomping on peanuts. Two of the trainers came over to scrape the goop off the bottom of my sneaker. It would have been a clear violation to have competed with that stuck onto my sneaker, since it might keep me inside my hexagon a split second longer should I fall outside the perimeter.

It really made me grin, all those fans with their foam thumbs thinking that we trained as hard as boxers, except maybe for the jumping rope, considering we'd let so many gimps into the competition.

At the sound of the bell I was a bit disoriented and nearly got pinned instantly, the good thing was that Koko pulled his thumb off at the count of three, when in fact this competition was for the count of four. Boy did he have egg on his face. Not that I was any better. I was flabbergasted myself and didn't have the smarts to take that as a clear chance to steal the initiative.

My job was to build the fans' hopes, which wasn't so difficult being the heavily favored. With so many people pulling for me this time I was supposed to make it look really good and then about seven or eight minutes into it take the fall.

That was the plan.

Mungo had that lousy gleam about him when he knew he was going to win, but beaming even more so. He really got his jollies from betting.

With only a few seconds from having the match go down as a draw, I leaned into Koko who wobbled the other way letting me squeeze his thumb, just enough to get him for the pin. The place went nuts. No sooner than I tossed my arms into the air did Mungo offer me his 'I'll chew your head off' snarl. His goons stood and followed me discreetly. Mungo certainly didn't need the crowd thinking he'd had anything crooked going on. Lulu lunged for my neck but missed me. Two of his other goons tailed me down the aisle and I made a reversal, circled passed one of the gimp matches then, when I saw Koko, I grabbed him for a moment, using him as a human shield and darted the other way.

Luz was nowhere in sight. I kept my eyes peeled, but with my lousy vision I could hardly see anyway. My sputtering heart seemed as if it would burst through my chest. I screamed out her name, but she didn't answer, though Lulu sneered. I suppose he thought I was taunting him.

Something else must have happened because the next thing I knew it was Mungo running for cover, but I was still trapped in the midst of it. Fists of fury swung about, programs, corndogs and lightweights went flying. The betting booth closed its window, and the angry mob pounded it.

The Farmer brothers timbered to the floor and became trampolines. Koko bounced off Burt's belly.

It was the rowdy old lady who'd been to the other matches the one who tackled the Indian man that saved me. She tripped Lulu with her cane and I escaped out the back.

The next day I woke up with a tremendous headache worse than any hangover. By mistake I even opened the refrigerator in pursuit of aspirins. On the bottom middle shelf was a half-eaten apple and a crumpled napkin. When I turned around I was startled by Luz.

"Sit down," Luz said and pushed the chair to me.

"My head feels like it's going to explode," I said.

"Good, you deserve it after what you pulled," Luz said and looked at the couch, but wouldn't sit.

"Why are you being like that?"

"You screwed him and after everything he did for you."

"Wait a second, where is this coming from?"

"It's not even the money so much. But now you've ruined his name."

"Well, let me tell you his name isn't exactly Mister Magoo."

"What's that supposed to mean?"

"He's a freaking goon."

"Don't you dare say that? He's got a great heart."

"Look, I'd really love to fight about this but my head is splitting. Please, tell me where the aspirins are and I'll let you beat me up all you want."

"You're a real jerk, you know that."

"What pisses you off is that I'm blunt and I'm not glitterati like the guys you hang out with."

"Let's drop this."

"No, I don't think so. I'm on a roll. You know, we all want to do big things. You just don't like it that I know your little secret."

"You better square yourself with Mungo."

"Not that, I mean I know about your dog detail."

"Shut up."

"What's the big deal? You've seen me selling stuffed animals, books on the street. I thumb-wrestle for a buck, and best of all, until like two months ago, I lived with my Mom."

She walked away from me, but I grabbed her wrist.

"Get off."

"I want to ask you something and I want an answer. Did you enjoy sleeping together?"

"I don't know."

"Well, I do and I can't keep pretending it didn't happen. We need to face it like mature adults. I'm not going to hate you if you don't want me, but I have to know because I can't go on this way."

"I don't have an answer for you."

"Where are you going?"

"I need to get some air and think," Luz said hand on the doorknob.

"Let's go to the park. We like it there."

"Benny, don't be so pushy. I don't know what I want."

"Pardon me for caring about you, but I can't stop thinking of us."

"There is no us. Not that way."

"Maybe we can go back. Have a few dates or something."

"Benny, I know too much. I think I need a break."

"From what, our friendship?"

"Yes."

"Things can build from friendship."

"If that's what we both want."

"And you're so sure?"

"One of these days you are going to fly."

"And so will you."

"I hope so."

It was the saddest thing she had yet said to me. She had a vacant look and her shoelaces were undone. I bent down to tie them, but she broke free. And I let her go. I was happy she didn't take anything along with her, but that didn't stop me from worrying. Luz was not tied to me. That she made clear. In an odd way I'd wished she left me a note instead of confronting me. A folded leaf of paper I could return to, reread and reinterpret to fit my mood.

I didn't even bother to get a glimpse of her from the fire escapes. I denied myself that last indulgence, to trick myself into believing I had willpower. Really, I didn't want to cry.

Breath of Fresh Despair

Our toothbrushes kissed and I stared at them because it epitomized us on so many levels: circumstantial, spiritual, sexual; two hermetically aligned plastic devices, bristles enmeshed, the perfect forget-me-not. I stuffed her toothbrush inside a box of her tampons encroaching onto my side of the medicine cabinet. I remembered how rough she brushed her poor teeth polishing her gums with such force she spat blood every time she was done.

**

A couple of days later, while I felt down in the dumps, Brig stopped by my book table. Yep, I had to keep busy so the books came out of hibernation and I returned to the same spot. Brig offered a nonpartisan smile while thumbing through Reuben Fine's Undermining Sicilian Defense's Dragon Variation that he conveniently found cracked open and upright. I knew he'd eventually be back and somebody should be happy.

"Bravo, you did it," Brig said.

"Yeah, well with Luz gone I've had lots of time on my hands."

"No shit. Sorry about that."

"Such is life."

"Let's get a change of scenery," Brig said, dog-earing a page. "I'm always crowding your office, humor me by checking out mine."

"Now is not the time. I'm a cadaver."

"Nonsense, follow me."

We bussed it downtown because Brig refused to take the subway. One time he'd been stalled because some nimrod passenger fainted. The front car snailed into the station, but Brig was in the penultimate car and had to march, single file, with the other passengers, through a secret passageway in the tunnel. The stench from the cruddy tracks, the rats, and the oil drip didn't bother him as much as the rubbing of sweaty arms and the superfluous kicking of shoes from the exit-hatch escapees. He never wanted to put himself in that bind so he walked or bussed wherever he was going. Plus, the subways weren't conducive to reading, aside from junk paper blurbs. That part made sense to me.

Brig pulled the stop cord on almost every block just to be annoying even though we were on an express. I twirled my finger close to my ear so the passengers might realize I was accompanying a nut. Birds of a feather. We got off in the Village and headed toward Washington Square

Park. As we passed through the arches, a bunch of street performers did back flips. Students, tourists, burnouts, hipsters and yuppie couples pushing funky-ass strollers that could've been taken for Italian scooters surrounded the street dancers, but most flew the scene once the hat went around. I tossed whatever change sat in my pocket because it took guts to do the crazy shit they were doing and I bet none of the performers had any disability insurance. Plus, my heart went out to them since I was a member of the street-hustling brotherhood.

The chess folk hid in the back of the park behind picnic benches, past the dog pen. Nobody seemed to fit the description of a typical chess player; they all seemed to be hustlers who might as well have been shooting craps or playing the ponies. Some looked slick enough to peel hubcaps off your car or sell junk electronics out of a van, I don't know, maybe that's what chess players looked like nowadays. Brig nodded to a couple of them as we went over. I became engrossed in one particular game in which two scrawny guys moved their pawns lightning quick, occasionally toppling each other's pieces then quickly stood them back upright. No smirks allowed. Their eyes hawked each other's Kings and when the one guy's flag dropped from his clock I could have sworn his opponent was reaching into his pocket for a piece. It turned out to be a browning banana.

The fresh smell of manure filled the air, teasing me into imagining the aroma of my favorite First Growth, Chateau Margaux. A table by the other end opened up and two Russians, who just finished their grudge match, dumped their pieces in a leather case and went off bickering over their game. I sat at the table, tossed my head back and took a deep sniff of the fertilizer, trying to go through my relaxation exercise. It had been months since I had made the effort to build upon my meditational craft, and even though my pockets were lined with more cash than ever before, I still felt depleted.

"How about a quickie?" Brig said parking opposite me.

"Give me a moment," I said.

"I won't take your milk money this time."

"No, you just startled me."

"Still thinking about Luz?"

"Yup."

"I'll spot you a rook," he said, removing the piece from the board.

This time Brig didn't have it so easy. His nose flared, revealing his ironclad consternation, as well as his swaying nose hairs. I tied up the center of the board because he loved his bishops and that was the only way to stump their mobility. I'm not even sure what I did. Some ghostly grand master guided my pieces, launching my knight to a critical post.

My knight had morphed into an octopus whose tentacles clamped down into all of Brig's sensitive squares. My opponent's meager horses cowered in the corner.

I was afraid to move anything. The mysterious lynchpin resided somewhere on the board. A simple, unintentional putz move and everything would tumble. Pawns falling like bowling pins. But even if I finally took Master Brig, it meant zero, in the grand scheme of things. Maybe I was too preoccupied with Luz. I'd never felt so empty. Not even that time I was waiting for the rain to let up during Aunt Chloe's graduation ceremony. A lightning bolt wouldn't have stirred me, better if it had pierced through my heart.

Brig's belly rumbled though he sank his teeth deep into his unwrapped schwarma. A smarmy twosome dropped by for a close-up and muddled commentary. They traded elbows and even dared suggestions until Brig roared at them. They slithered away.

"What sign are you?" I asked.

"Libra," he said.

"Just wondering."

"What about?"

"You bark like a Leo," I said. "Thought maybe you were –"

"A lion. You believe that crud."

"Not really. But don't you sometimes think of what lies beyond the unknown?"

"Not when I'm playing."

"Maybe we should play later."

"You're not slipping away that easily. No sir, you're going to have to crush me."

"Let's call it a draw. My head's mush," I said, offering my hand.

"Too freaking bad. Suck it up. C'mon wipe the board with me, I dare you."

Brig brought his knees up, crouching into a wrecking ball. He took his time, rubbing his free hand underneath his scruffy chin.

"I can't take it," I said.

"Hang in there and finish the job."

"I can't take it that she up and left me."

"Ugh, Luz again."

"I know she had feelings for me, too, but she was too chicken to face it."

"Join the club," Brig said.

"What?"

"That's right, I used to date Luz, too," Brig said.

"I don't believe it."

"Why would I lie?"

The thought of it, Luz with him, and all that schwarma and Tahini sauce dribbling from his mouth, turned my stomach. I wouldn't believe it. And then I couldn't keep from believing it. Time hadn't taught me anything about women and everything about being a sucker, a pawn in the game of life.

"Don't get so bent out of shape. For what it's worth, I know what you are going through," Brig said.

"What the hell, how come you never said anything?"

"When you told me you fell for Luz, I guess I didn't want to dig up the past. Nothing lasts forever. So much going for me back then. Look how far I've fallen down the totem pole."

Brig blundered his bishop and I missed the chance to snag it.

"I hate you this way," he said. "So I'm going to share with you places she might be."

"You think I don't know her."

"You want her back, don't you?"

"Of course."

"Well then, you need to listen to what I'm telling you. I know. After all, I was with her longer, almost a year."

"Good for you. So where do I start?"

"Don't hold me to this but there was this guy Kramnik, who she was always buying jewelry from. You know those turquoise stones she wears around her neck. Kramnik is the spazola who made those things. Sold them like hotcakes. Believe me, they weren't cheap. She spent time with him because she thought he was going to be a great pop artist. He has a cabin and some vintage canoes by his lake house upstate. Maybe she's camped up there. You might find him at the Kiev Diner, that's where he hangs out."

Brig returned to his position on the board. Unable to contain his fibrillating upper lip, he punched his lone rook and queen into a last-effort ambush, thereby neglecting all other corners of the board. So I plugged the hole he yearned to charge through. No quick, slam bam checkmates on my watch, not this time. My pawn chain supported by an octopus blunted his hope for counterattack.

Brig sketched the air to comprehend the aftermath of the inevitable rank and file plunge that would expel his rook/queen combo. He cut into my pawn chain, but as I defrocked his bishop, Brig's cheeks deflated. He fixed on the cul-de-sac where his rook/queen tandem would fall, leaving him no other choice but to resign.

He wiped his hands on his trousers before offering me his hand.

***

Luz had many shades of gray and it bugged me that the more I learned the less I seemed to know about her. It reminded me of this girl from elementary school named Nariko, who I'd actually met in kindergarten Bible Studies camp, where we sang "Michael Rowed the Boat Ashore" and jumped through sprinklers on the back-lawn-cum-chapel.

I'd known Nariko for so many years, ten in fact, that by the time I'd been promoted into eighth grade, I realized I knew nothing about the girl. A boy named Thomas was the only new student that Fall in my sixth grade class, a transplant from Flushing. We became friends. We happened to walk the same path home every day. So little by little we got to know each other.

Around the same time, he started to become pretty chummy with Nariko. Not that I'd paid much attention to it, since I was focused on winning the batting crown on my baseball team. One day out of the blue I got in an argument with Thomas about Nariko because he claimed he knew more about her than I did. I'd known her for ten years. Who did he think he was when he hardly knew her beyond a trimester?

It turned out that, other than my knowledge of the multitude of dorky hairstyles she'd gone through, courtesy of the school photos I was in possession of, I really knew practically zippo about Nariko. I was even mistaken about the street she lived on even though I passed it when I headed to the ball field with my dad. She lived on Exeter, not Fleet.

Thomas knew which boys she liked, having seen her scribbled sweethearts inside her marble notebook. He knew that underneath the secret compartment to her Hello Kitty pencil case she kept a photograph of her little brother and the lyrics to U2's Joshua Tree.

I'd known her for all those years and had been to all her birthday parties, bowling at Woodhaven Lanes, McDonald's on Metropolitan, the roller skating shindig behind the now defunct gas tanks on Grand Avenue, I'd even been to that infamous make-out party while her folks were off celebrating their fifteenth anniversary in Tahiti. The whole place was one big incestuous tangle of arms and legs and I ended up playing ping pong the whole night. Nariko had her very first French kiss that night with Thomas. He didn't even tell me about it till years later.

I worried that some mook lurking out there, some Thomas, was going to take my place with Luz and rub my face in it.

I killed the afternoon in the Kiev Diner just as Brig suggested and studied the crayon sketch of Kramnik that Brig was kind enough to produce. It was nice to know the boy genius was equally inept at

symmetry and shading as I was. It was highly improbable that a wild
boar was coming to dine at Kiev, but I sat anyway. A good many fatsoes
wolfed down blitzes, sour cream dripping off their chins, preferring to
save their napkins to wipe the sweat off their brows. A mandarin orange
glow beat through the thick, smudged glass and the waitress kept giving
me a dirty look when I stuck my mug out for another coffee refill. I
ordered a second muffin because I felt bad. I was the only shnook, in the
whole place, who wasn't eating Ukrainian.
I flipped through a stack of rag newspapers to pass the time. There were
so many nifty sex ads that I'd sort of became addicted to reading the
personals and had practically gotten the nerve to call a really kinky one
daring to lick yogurt off her nipples.

The waitress swung by again and gave me a dirty look and I pulled
my knees together and tried not to disturb the bulge rumbling
downstairs.

I almost split for the day when Kramnik strolled in, took a seat by the
window and grabbed his napkin from the table and stuffed it into his
collar. He'd been there a whopping two minutes and a tray of food was
brought over to him, a plate of blintzes, Polish sausages, and some other
greasy potato dumpling crap.

He shoveled the food into his face, grunting and groaning as if he was
bench-pressing a thousand pounds. The folds in his neck wriggled as the
clumps of food wobbled down. The sausages seemed like they might
even bust through his neck. The napkin under his chin and the utensils in
his hands were about the only things that made it clear he wasn't a wild
boar, maybe.

It got so gross after a while I bit the bullet and went to him. Maybe
he'd have the decency to drop his fork if we were talking business.

"Can I help you?" he said licking the sour cream off his thumb.

"I was told to talk to you about a certain young woman."

"A pretty little girl."

"Her name is Luz."

"What do you want with her?"

"It's personal, where can I find her?"

He lay down his knife and fork. His dark eyes grew wide, pensive,
biblical. He reminded me briefly of a fat deacon who gave early morning
masses from the old school.

"Forget about her. She's a tease."

"Now look, if you have any idea where she is I need to know."

"How should I know? She only bugs me when she wants something.
Who told you I know her?"

"I can't say."

"So valiant. What do I get in return?"

I slipped him a twenty dollar-bill. He didn't even bother to peek and stuffed it into his shirt pocket.

"The last I heard she was fine."

"When was that?"

"A week ago."

"You were with her."

"And a room full of eager idiots. A mixed bag guys and girls; an art gallery opening."

The idea of Luz cozying up to this slob even in a purely platonic way made me sick to my stomach. Nothing about him said artist, if anything his drugstore cologne screamed asshole.

"Any particular haunts I might find her."

"Robert Mann."

He then got red in the face and began choking on some food. His chest was pounding and he sank his head forward and waved his hand like a blind man swimming through a sea of plankton.

Two waiters scurried over, but shook their fingers at each other. The cashier yelled for the manager and a clatter rang out of the kitchen, a dozen or so plates shattered onto the marble floor.

Everybody stared at me as if I was a long lost swami materializing from a bottle of potion. Kramnik was bleary-eyed and begging me to help him.

"So you're going to tell me where Luz is?" I said.

His face purpled and he tossed the dishes off the table.

"Where is she?"

He finally nodded. So I went behind the big slob, wrapped my arms around his globulous frame and pumped my fists into his chest. The third time he coughed it up. The sausage chunk shot into the air, sailed over the table and landed in an old woman's coffee.

Kramnik wiped his sweaty face and the wait staff clapped.

"My doctor's been busting my hump to stop with the Kovbasa and I think this must be a sign."

"Chew more slowly."

"She's been house-sitting for somebody in Chelsea. Go to the Robert Mann Gallery Opening tomorrow night. Ask for Chula. That's what they call her."

***

The gallery was a real meat market. This well-coifed Euro trash guy flashed his stainless steel, Swiss Automatic Bulgari to a couple of

Brazilian models. The scene was totally foreign and it intimidated me. Nobody was into the art and for good reason. It was junk. There was no coherent theme: video installations, mousetraps glued to a giant oak tag, a list of serial rapists typed out and entitled Scumbags. I'm not an art critic, but this was a pathetic showing. Truthfully, the characters and gadabouts piqued my curiosity much more. I stayed for a few cubes of pepperjack cheese, wheat crackers, and a swig or two of ungodly plastic cups of white plonk, New Zealand Sauvignon blanc. The essence of that breed is described as cat's pee on a gooseberry bush, according to certain connoisseurs – damn straight.

When the opening was winding down I realized she wasn't coming, but I poked my head into a few other venues. The same art whores seemed to comet-tail through gallery town. I didn't stick around long just poked my head in to see if Luz was anywhere. I even checked registries, but no such luck.

Charlie gave me a buzz and begged me to go to a hole-in-the-wall nudie bar with him. First round was on him, so I agreed. We got there by nine as a plate of atomic wings arrived on the bar. Twenty-five cents a pop, drafts were still two dollars. "Luxury," as the old boy liked to say. Not too shabby except for the merchandise.

This one stripper wouldn't leave me alone all because I bought her a lousy drink. What a Herculean mistake. And she wouldn't shut up. Kept jabbering on horoscope nonsense and that she had somebody building her a new cabinet for all the shoes she owned. Took one look at her lime green pumps and nodded.

"How about a dance sugar?" she asked.

"Sounds great, but I kind of promised somebody else," I said.

"Good then, save the best for last."

"Tempting, but I'm going to chill for now."

She kept hounding though and scoped me the whole while she was on stage twirling the pole and saw that I didn't make a move for anybody. When she came back she told me she'd make it worth my while, her big glassy eyes, frazzled, distant as if gazing beyond the room, beyond the doors. A desperate pleasure usurped my sensibility.

I knew I'd regret it.

Charlie was teasing me and loving it because, according to him, even though it was a total dive chock full of telemarketers, what he called pathetic accuses for strippers, that belonged on the other end of a telephone selling credit card services and Ginso Knives, he was dirty and knew with a wave of a few measly dollars he could have his way with practically anyone in the place. We were only supposed to stay for a beer, some wings and a few laughs.

Melody, as I heard the DJ announcing her to return to stage, implored me to wait by the bar. She confronted one of the bouncers, and after a shouting match that seemed as if she would end up punched in the face, was able to skip her catwalk on stage in order to make good on the promise that I didn't want in the first place, to get a private dance with her, un-chaperoned, off somewhere in the back.

When I got out of the john, she was waiting for me. Finally, I took her up on her offer for a lap dance. Pin another merit badge on my breast pocket. She led me to the back room, past the bar and the john, behind a beaded curtain. She shut the door and shimmied out of her bikini top. Her breasts were plump, but sagging and she wasted no time stuffing them in my face. Her nipples were moist and tasted like fruitless yogurt. I thought of the personal ad from earlier then felt queasy.

Amidst the dusty glow peppering down from the crooked overhead bulb she recognized me; I too had the funny feeling I knew her from somewhere. She snaked her legs around my hips dipping back so her golden hair swept onto the floor.

Her belly wriggled and I stroked her inny button.

"Tommy," she whispered into my ear with smoky breath and began petting the back of my neck.

She ran her fingers under my shirt, tickling my chest hair. When she finally pulled her hair out of the ponytail, letting it spill over her shoulders, it took a while, but after I looked beyond the puffy eyes and mask of makeup, it became more evident that she was indeed, by some miracle of hyper-acceleration space-time and dye-job, Sara Gonzalez, the girl I had had the biggest crush on in the world, many moons ago, as a puny dork back at Our Lady of Perpetual Hope. The one that had snuck down into the crook of the steps beneath the convent, hiding with me from the other kids, during a game of hide and seek. We sat there tangled, her legs wrapped around mine, mirroring the vines coiling the drainage pipe all the way up to the roof – Sister Mary Donovan's habit and Sister Dorothy's tracksuit hanging out to dry formed a canopy to give us the added protection we needed from being caught.

With clasped fingers, we prayed together to the Virgin Mary that we wouldn't get caught, fearing if word broke out about us in this compromising position we would be made into laughing stocks.

In secret, I prayed with vim and vigor to St. Anthony that I might find the courage to explore what delicious mystery lay beneath Sara's pleated skirt, but to no avail. I was too frightened to delve the depths of her moistened flesh. Her tender arms cloaked around my lanky body, my face buried in her wavy brown hair. It smelled delicious, a sumptuous mélange of strawberries and flour, from helping her mother, sometimes after school, at the local bakery.

She was the first girl I ever fantasized about when I used to play with my shrimpy pecker, back in elementary school. I moaned her name underneath the sheets and comforter, late at night, after my parents had fallen asleep.

I had always been too chicken to dip my tongue into her mouth. She soon would garner quite a reputation for being the makeout queen. Thomas, that bastard, who made out with Nariko beat me to it again and kissed Sara.

Our hearts throbbed in unison as the shuffling feet above us drew near.

"Do you think that you can remove them?" little Sara asked me, gazing beyond the rectory's bushes.

"What?" I said, looking out for nuns.

"Those lines. I mean, once they've covered a piece of your heart."

"Oh, that, well, I don't know. I'm not sure we really get these lines in the first place. For one thing, wouldn't we feel it? Take my cousin for instance. He coughs this nasty brown goo, after he smokes. Two packs a day."

"How old is he?"

"Twenty, but when he coughs he sounds like he's going to cough up his lungs. See, I could picture some lines over his heart, but you."

"You think it's a sin to smoke?"

"Nah, but health wise, I'm sure it messes you up, like a big black belt strapping your aorta."

"But if those lines smudge your heart all over, it's as if your naked. You can die of coldness."

"It's just a story."

"So what makes you so sure you don't get them for having dirty thoughts?"

Back then if it had all been true what the nuns had told us about excessive masturbation I would have morphed into a gorilla, my palms, my arms, my whole body would've been that hairy and my heart would've been as dark as coal. This sort of thing I surmised she was driving at, not that I would've spit those words aloud, not to her. It never dawned on me that perhaps there was something else she was alluding to, bewildering her fledgling consciousness.

"Maybe cold hearts need mittens," I said. "To me the heart doesn't look anything like the candy box."

"No you're right, not from our textbook."

118

That was the closest I came to doing anything with her. Sara left school midway through the seventh grade, for reasons that were never made clear, although rumor spread that she hooked into a bad crowd and messed with drugs. Another was that she got knocked up.

During senior year of high school I'd spotted her on a crowded subway headed toward Jackson Heights. By the time I'd elbowed my way through the crowd she was on the platform. The door had shut between us and I barked her name. She turned to palm the door and I pressed my fingers against the glass shadowing her hand.

Often I thought about her whenever eating donuts or cupcakes. For a while, I searched for her, questioning different bakeries in nearby towns. I flipped a picture of Sara to whoever was behind the counter, but again and again they tossed it back to me with a shrug, the picture smeared with powder and icing.

I'd sniff the picture, thinking of her.

One time I even went on a blind date because the girl I was set up with happened to be a Latina Sara and I hoped serendipity would finally be on my side.

Now, she was before me spreading more or less naked, her legs jutting high above my head as though she were an air traffic controller waving signals to a troubled plane.

The song finished and she was slow to slide off my lap. I pried her off me nearly getting to my feet, but she wouldn't let go. The bouncer began pounding on the door until she informed him that I would be getting another dance.

"Really, that's Okay," I said, tucking in my shirt. "I'll get you a drink outside."

"You don't want to be with me?"

"No, it's not that. I'm beat and I need to be up super early."

"So we party tonight," she said, putting her arms around my shoulders. "We're only young once, Tommy."

The dark pouches under her eyes and the sagginess round her neck made me realize she wasn't Sara. She must have been through a lot, but she definitely wasn't Sara. Maybe I wanted to believe this or maybe I wanted to get my second chance and make up for lost time. I stood and didn't know what to do with my hands so I linked my thumbs through empty belt straps. Sad part of it was that I had this cheery feeling being wanted even though I wasn't exactly who she wanted. I was all mixed up.

I wondered who the real Tommy must have been and if he realized what he had done.

The next song splashed out of the speakers and with a sudden burst of energy she began pulsating to the beat. With dizzied thrusts she rocked her body on my lap, lifting my shirt and flopped her flabby belly against my flesh. I tucked my hands by her shoulder blades more to keep her from intruding past my comfort zone, but she was slippery with sweat.

She licked my earlobes and I crawled back, but was trapped in a wooden chair, not a leather couch, which would otherwise give me more room to squirm. This bare bones dive left me defenseless.

She leaned into my lips and let me graze her gloss. It smelled like bubblegum. I even tried to kiss her but she pulled back. Then she slipped off me and sobbed between my legs, mascara ran down her cheeks.

"I stocked the fridge. There's pork chops and beer and lots of ice-cream, chocolate, pistachio. It'll be like old times," she said, using my pants as a face towel.

"Look, I think you're terrific but you're mistaking me for somebody else."

"You're a prick. You know that. Why haven't you called?"

She wiggled back into her panties. I was two seconds from going home with her just to appease this cockeyed mirage she was having of me, but that would've served no good purpose and I was disheartened seeing her this way.

As I was tipping her she dug through her purse, pulling out pictures of her two boys, scruffy things in buzzcuts beaming churlish grins, neither of which looked anything at all like her.

"So how about it, I'll fry those pork chops for breakfast."

Off went my jean jacket, I draped it around her shoulders. She still quivered.

When we left the back room she huddled close to me by the bar, rubbing my leg until I finished my sudsy beer. Charlie made goofy faces till she grew cross, tore off the jacket, balled it and chucked it at him.

On the way out, I wondered what would've happened if I'd made out with Sara on the steps of the convent. Where she was and whatever happened to that picture I had of her that smelled of powdered sugar.

***

I took a long hot shower after that, scrubbed my body with a hard sponge. To think I was inches away from going home with her because I felt sorry for her, sorry for myself. We could've cried our mittens out together.

I didn't towel off but walked naked from the bathroom and looked at the postcards Luz and I had hung on the wall, from our separate trips abroad. I'd never met anybody before who'd had virtually the same type of experiences as I'd had traveling. Who looked for the same type of adventure, laid back, random, a walk through Rome in an afternoon and then spend the rest of the time sitting in cafes sipping cappuccinos, reading books, and earnestly trying to blend in with the crowd.

What got me, though, was that at least half a dozen times Luz asked me to take off with her. She'd mention it on our bus trips to nowhere. Why didn't I go with the flow one time? Had I, all would have been well and we'd be off somewhere, pitching a tent, trying to catch freshwater fish with our bare hands or maybe poking at them with a stick.

All I had to do was take the initiative, sounded like a broken record the more I thought of it. Sounded like Brig hammering in that mantra with regards to counterattacks for black and white; my problem was that I sunk back too long. Wasn't that why Luz left?

I mean, if it hadn't been for that stupid doll we would never have become intimate.

I peed at least ten times because I kept drinking water. Even tried doing the dishes the way Luz used to without rubber gloves because they left marks on her wrists and she hated the smell of rubber, but the one knob was so damn hot I burned myself. Water sprayed off the bottom of the pot and zapped me off the chest, pectoral flambé. Maybe I shouldn't have been doing dishes topless.

Comfort of Rain

After a short sabbatical, I returned to work to find that some protégé had taken my place, Whatshisface. Mungo grit his teeth when he passed me by, but didn't show any gum. I was happy he didn't break my legs. Instead of physical punishment, he removed me from the thumb-wrestling arena. He wouldn't let me tend to the monkeys either because he knew I loved this.

When we came face to face he appeared on the brink of reprimanding me. He swallowed back his words, said nothing and his understated detachment hurt me more because I knew I'd screwed him as Luz said. Mungo's jowls, plastered into a curve of dismay, brought to mind the disappointment my dad had when I retired my baseball cleats. I'd grown comfortable quitting.

I knew I wasn't going to make it through the day, but I wanted a bit of closure as hokey as it sounded. I passed the old stomping grounds where my furry, dart-slinging pals were, but when I got there the room exuded a stifled aura through the Plexiglas. Many new monkey faces, and no Thelonious. He'd been sold to perform in a traveling Stomp show. In a way, I was glad for him, but my thoughts sputtered off to the past, remembering how he'd passed his celery baton to me. I let him down too.

Truthfully, I hadn't the foggiest idea what next step to take. Again, I dwelled on failure even though I supposedly triumphed, making the pin. The fact was the result bordered on Pyrrhic Victory. I'd won, but lost. I enjoyed what I'd been doing and wasn't allowed to continue. What did I want to do? Off the top of my head, I'd always wanted to pick grapes from the craggy slopes of the Rhone valley or in Northern Spain, the Priorat. Maybe I wanted to soil my hands because it reminded me of the infield of my youth.

The travel bug had bitten me again. And, I thought of Luz discouraging me from taking sojourns only to return home. She made her point, but wouldn't know she'd be the impetus behind my flight. That's what she said. I would fly. She was right. Luz left behind her family, survived, and was evolving. What was keeping me from turning a new page? I'd start afresh, a reconfigured life. I could go anywhere.

First, I had to raise money. I planned on unloading my books. Then there were the loose ends to tie, find somebody to take over my sublease agreement so that I could pocket my part of the security deposit.

I had a tough time finding anybody to pickup my sublease. Seems the people who'd responded to the flyers I'd posted were less together, less sedentary than me. One even thought I'd inquired on a house-sitter. How could anybody be so obtuse? Then again, I recalled the nutty retired dentist who wanted to sell me a trunk instead of renting me his apartment. Vintage Manhattan bred idiosyncrasy – a dying breed.

Since I couldn't get anybody on such short notice to take the apartment, I had to break the lease agreement and forfeit the security deposit. From book sales and coins scraped together I'd collected barely enough to get myself across state lines let alone on a plane to France. The king-sized clearance sale continued. I let the books go for any price. Make one up, I dared browsers. I didn't sell much. The Age of the Enlightenment for a quarter, A Portrait of an Artist, probably a second edition, bargained down to forty-two cents.

It had begun to drizzle but I sat in repose flipping through William James and though I was covering the quest of the pathfinder, I kept looping the prescient declaration, "that the masses of men lead quiet lives of desperation." This was always happening to me, jumbling the meanings and ideologies of thinkers, swapping the words of Jung with Freud, Milton with Marlowe, and in this case James with Thoreau.

Pebbles of rain pelted down and I scratched my head over what to stuff under the tarp first, the French Existentialists or the Neo-Platonists. Hmm, would this be an example of procrastination or over analysis?

A scarecrow of a tree barely hung over me, but like a broken umbrella's spokes, the flimsy branches rode up in the wind. Rain trickled down my cheeks. Two hours withered by, the same book in my hands, and I kept circling the same fragments. On the page they were complete thoughts, sentences, properly punctuated, but in my head they unraveled.

Some kids looking for nudie magazines kept bugging me. I was on the lookout for Brig, I wanted to clear things up with him and see if he'd bumped into Luz.

I was also getting kind of melancholy. The wet corduroy feeling invaded my grape-picking inspiration. I saw the golden slopes of France as a mirage. My tongue burned with thirst and my ears rang. Random electric guitar chords plucked in my head, the Zeppelin I'd been listening to earlier in the morning Black Dog. I've heard that John Paul Jones was inspired to write Black Dog based on the Muddy Water's tune Electric Mud. I don't think Zeppelin filling my head had anything to do with my changing mood swing. I strummed air arpeggios to stress my steadfast belief.

I closed shop and lugged my boxes burdened with books over to the nearest bench across the street. There I took refuge and fussed with the cardboard flaps until it stayed shut. I brushed a clump of wet leaves off the bench partially exposing the initials R.B. A strange coincidence. I'd once carved those very initials on a tree. They stood for Ruby Brooks, an imaginary girlfriend I invented to prove to my buddy Thomas that I wasn't any wuss and it didn't mean shit that he'd made out with Nariko while I played ping pong in her basement. I'll admit Ruby Brooks was a rather silly combo, but what can I tell you it just slipped off my tongue.

Somebody had left a bag of crumpled bread by the foot of the bench. Six pigeons waddled by my sneaker so I tossed them crumbs. The fattest ones gobbled first. Fat pigeons like go-getters pounced on opportunity – the bread of life. Bubbles fizzled from vents in my sneaker. For a moment, I rode the wave of meditational triumph, concentrating on the water bubbles. Then the breeze blew some soggy leaves making me realize the damp coldness of my socks and pants clinging to my body. A dark orange leaf, colored and coiled into a burnt burrito was carried by the wind, till it met a nearby stream where it drifted toward the sewer. The leaf choked through the narrow opening.

Then I felt a bony hand grab my wrist. I flinched, feeling like one of those Devonian-age deep sea fish prodded for the first time by a boob fisherman.

***

Nobody approached me in the park, my hermitage. You'd think that I could deal with it, what with people constantly poking their grimy fingers all over my books. Sometimes I got into good conversations and the day flew by, but other times I got stuck with a crackpot who'd hang around all day long, the Brigs of this mudball, pestering about nothing in particular, just because they were lonely and figured I had nothing better to do. Well, I was out making a living, however meager it seemed and, sadly enough, really had nothing better to do.

After a while, I realized that was only part of the equation. The other part had to do with these transient symbiotic relationships I'd bumbled into. I'd become a facilitator of and a participant in the lives of stragglers. They'd tell me things about their lives that I didn't always need to know but I never told them to shut up. Others kept coming back because they happened to find coupons napping inside some of my merchandise, fifty cents off Rice Crispies, a free jar of Dijon mustard when you bought a whole Boar's Head ham, half price cat food. Word had gotten out about my coupon smorgasbord. Actually, they had all been my bookmarks, but when browsers flipped through my books and found a freebie they had no problem slipping it into their pocket, and I never made an issue out of it. This is what brought them back a second, a third, a twenty-fifth time, because I was putz enough not to charge them when they hit pay dirt.

Whatever the reason, I enjoyed the catch-as-catch-can games my customers played with me. It reminded me of my relationship with Luz. I got to know her in small portions. She wasn't a penguin, somebody who wanted to be stuck for life, any more than I was a buttoned-down conformist. Except that I wanted to be stuck with her.

I lifted my head, allowing a full frontal view of my widow's peak and was stunned to see it was the old lady from the arena again with her skinny cane. Good old reliable – one of my biggest fans, her trusty cane my salvation after the melee broke out during my last thumb-wrestling match. I don't know why she looked so old to me now. She certainly didn't look so waving her foam thumb, cursing at the top of her lungs.

Frazzled, but silent my mouth crinkled ajar. Water dripped down her uncovered forehead. She had no umbrella.

"Is that Helen on the cover?" she said. Her hand trembled, hanging onto her cane, for dear life. "Helen Carlson, the former first lady, is she on the front page?"

I hadn't the foggiest idea what she was referring to till I saw a Village Voice loafing on the far side of the bench. I swiped the soggy paper and offered it to her.

She grabbed it too hard and tore a promotional listing of upcoming performances at The Cutting Room.

"Ornette Coleman at Iridium," she said. "Give me a break, like I'm going to spend fifty bucks when I can see him for free under the stars at the Southstreet Seaport."

No argument there.

I almost fell in the love with the way the newsprint smudged on her fingers and how she didn't seem to give damn about the needless baptism spilling over us. I wanted to thank her for her support, for saving my ass. She had more to get off her chest.

"It didn't matter that she cut it. Bubba didn't notice, didn't give a crap."

"I'm not following you," I said.

"Don't you listen to the radio?" she said.

"Not really, not talk radio at least."

"Wake up. That's the hotbed of human interest."

"I'll remember that."

"No you won't"

I rather liked her bluntness. Her concern for the former first lady seemed personal. Was she acquainted? She leaned closer and I noticed by her cane's angle she was losing balance. She wobbled. And then before I had a chance to move she plopped onto my lap along with the paper. She squirmed around. Mortified, I threw my shoulders to the back of the bench. Her pink lipstick smeared above and below her lips and her heavy make-up melted down her cheeks. I remembered how she jumped on top of the Indian guy by Plex's waterfall, but I didn't get the sense she would pull that with me.

She actually seemed embarrassed to have slipped; I played it off like it was no big shakes.

I gave her a boost though her stubborn body bottomed back onto my lap. She clutched her cane as if about to plunge off a cliff. Finally, she raised herself from the bench and the chicken-scrawled message "I love you R.B" became fully visible.

"When I was a girl, around nineteen, I too had short hair. It was popular back then. They called it the boyish look."

"Really," I said, watching her pallid fingers tremble. She revealed her palm, the lifelines squashed together like so much dough.

"It's funny, both men and women want their hair short nowadays. Guess it's been that way for a while. Vincent thought Eighties Women were nuts. All those punky haircuts: Pat Benatar, Princess Diana, the late Diana made short hair fashionable in the eighties. Vincent couldn't take anything but shoulder-length hair on women," she said, eyes on my forehead. "I too wore it short back then. Vincent called me a dyke. He's was a God damn poet."

She sank into the bench and peered off, to nowhere. Her familiarity with eighties pop culture impressed me since that was my jovial era of Star Wars lunchboxes, Hi-C box drinks and cheesy video games with retarded graphics. And yet there was a murkiness to it though I lived through it. I could practically taste it but then there were all those pictures swimming through my mind that made it seem like a dream. My signature affliction, did I remember real events or only images I'd made of them?

For some reason, I saw her younger now. I pictured her wearing a Bon Jovi T-shirt, a red bandana wrapped around her head.

Her tone was soothing, almost syrupy but not saccharine. She stopped mentioning Helen. Had she forgotten why she originally wanted to look at my paper? Maybe the Helen thing was just a ploy to come over and talk.

The more I listened the more I thought about never having a decent conversation with my grandmother. My grandparents kicked the bucket when I was really young. I can't remember saying anything to any of them.

I never got satisfactory answers when I asked about my grandparents, beyond the fact that my father's mother died when my dad was only a boy. That was hardly the thing to tell a little kid, since I often wondered when my mother would die.

My mother's mother never came to visit. She only sent a fruitcake around the holidays. Apparently, she'd been to my baptism and maybe one other useless gathering. Most of my memory of her comes from the only picture of the two of us in which she was holding a giant sombrero to cover my naked ass scooting across her front lawn. I vaguely recall her spooning tapioca pudding from her bowl, offering me some when we visited her at the old folks' home.

There was a void within me, but I didn't know enough about my grandparents to feel the loss. Pain was nil without memories. Listening now, forgetting what I had originally come to the park for wasn't really killing time; I was making up the lost time that I never spent with my grandmother.

She probably needed someone more than I did. Her heavy, melting makeup couldn't hide her pain. The more we chatted, the more we laughed about things that only old army buddies might find amusing, the more I noticed her wispy smile. Never full, it only crinkled by her left cheek. There was a deep concern laden in her eyes watching the fat pigeons chomping away at the crumbs.

Seeing her pain made me feel a little better about myself even though I didn't exactly know what was eating at her. And yet she sat tall, with posture better than mine as I slouched on the weathered bench. Something of a Yoda, but maybe not quite as wrinkled or green, one could probably figure her age by counting the rings beneath her eyes, but as curious as I was, I tamed the urge. She told me that placing eighty-seven candles on a cake would have to be a fire hazard.

"Light them, but have an extinguisher by your side," I said.

We laughed.

"This is the life out here, selling dreams to people," she said.

"I never really thought of it that way."

"During the depression that's how people got by, books and movies."

We both chimed in "If you don't have a dream then how you gonna make a dream come true."

Ode to South Pacific, it was a bit corny, but cute.

"You know it's funny, my roommate met Carlson," I said.

"Helen?" she replied.

"No, Bubba. She met him. She even danced with him, the mambo. She's so amazing she could sweep anybody off his feet."

"Then why haven't you let her sweep you?" She said.

"Does it show?" I said staring at my sneakers.

"Your eyes finally lit up, talking about her."

"But she's just my friend. Nothing more."

"A friend is a lot. They say you only have one real friend your entire life, if you're lucky."

"That can't be true."

"You can bring a friend to your dark side."

For a moment, I drifted off to the trip I took senior year of college, my first trip abroad. Nobody knew me and I was glad to have a new beginning. All my bottled worries spilled out and I basked in the Tuscan splendor. A Puerto Rican exchange student gave me a sterling silver frog pendant on my birthday, and told me it was called Coqui, a good luck charm from San Juan. Then she made me a birthday cake.

She didn't even know me. Why was she nice? Just to be friendly. I hadn't celebrated a birthday like that in years. I hated the fuss. Somewhere along the way, I lost my ephemeral popularity, if I ever really had it. People slipped in and out of my life. Nobody to blame but me and I never did anything about it, but here this adorable art history student, who knew next to nothing about me, made such a difference, boosting my belittled view of humanity. She slipped away because I didn't know how to keep up. There's a brief moment when I have a ridiculous urge to share my boundless love and then I think too much, the moment slides by and there's not an ounce of soul left in me. I'm just flesh and bones. I'm fruitless.

Sometimes at night just before I fall asleep I drift to a carefree past, which, come to think of it, wasn't that long ago, but it seems to have withered to a joke.

She slid toward the end of the bench, giving me the first impression she was ready to move along.

"I'm going away," I said, "To figure things out."

"Well, I hope you have a good trip."

"Actually, I'm not so sure I'd call it a trip. I'm going overseas, but I may not return. I've seen enough around here for now."

"You're still young, no need to rush into anything. You could be back here before you know it."

"I don't think so, but I need to make it on my own."

"That's brave of you."

"You don't sound convinced."

"I'm not the one who needs convincing here. It sounds to me like you've run up against something that you don't want to face."

"What makes you say that?"

"Not to pry. Really, it's none of my business. I'm always told I'm butting in too much as it is, even in my old age, but I get the sense you're still looking for permission to go."

"What permission do I need? I do as I please."

"Sure but what I meant is you're seeking permission from yourself. When I was a girl, I had this measly after-school job at a pet shop. I stuck price tags on kitty litter packages, scooped the bottom of the birdcage. You can't tell now but I used to be a smart cookie. I could've had a scholarship to a fancy prep school Uptown, but my father got very ill and the whole family, my sisters and my brothers, all had to pitch in. There I was with this mindless job with no time to study for my entrance exam and I wanted it so badly. I would've given anything–"

"And in the end you buckled down and came through," I interrupted.

"Not at all," she continued, "In fact, I failed miserably. Nobody was there for me, no shoulders to cry onto. Everybody was too tired busting their own humps. All my mother cared about was making sure food was on the table. All I wanted to do was write poetry and for a little while I did, late at night when nobody knew I was still up. It was bliss. Then one day it got to the point where my head filled with so much goop nothing came out right."

"That's happened to me too. Not with poetry but thoughts. They lodge in my head and won't come out. I've let so many opportunities slip past me it's disgusting. If you added up all the time I've wasted I could've given it to somebody really in need like an innocent death-row inmate."

She peered over her shoulder as if waiting for somebody to pass by that she wanted to dish about.

"I let my time slip by because I didn't give myself the permission I needed. I know this sounds crazy, but life is full of too many obstacles to deny yourself joy."

She let out a deep sigh.

I stared at the dampness on her face. Her eyes were pinkish, more so around the edges than they were earlier, purpling her pupils. Was she crying? It was hard to distinguish the rain on her face from the tears.

"Never let anybody mold you," she said, "you don't want to end up like me."

"What are you talking about? I hope I'll be as lively when I'm – I mean if I ever reach your age."

It made me sort of uneasy that I'd been loafing there using her misery earlier to make me feel better. Could she see me in my old age? Was Luz in my future? Both of us together, but separate; shrouding ourselves in our own brands of loneliness. For a moment, I found solace in a passage from James Thurber that basically said sex spoils healthy relationships. So my flubbed step into romance with Luz wasn't ruinous, but simply the way it had to be. The question then was how did I want it to be? I felt my thoughts billowing into the air. In the distance, some more leaves were getting sucked down the sewer.

My arm had been tucked by my side too long so I stretched it out, but was uncomfortable propping it up on the benchrest. My fingers squirmed as if to make a shadow puppet or swat at a fly. The situation called for neither. I perched my elbow on the bench's wooden slab, coiling my elbow so it fit snugly, right against the groove, Washington Square Park's answer to the old-fashioned pillories.

While she was lost in thought, I tried catching raindrops in my mouth.

"My husband Vincent ran off with a floozy. He was wearing his Hawaiian shirt, the one he wore on our honeymoon – carrying our luggage, a present from our fortieth wedding anniversary. Those damn Viagra pills. I never should have told him to get the prescription."

Just then, the sun, no more than a coppery speck, set in the sky. It softened the charcoal backdrop and once again, I saw her hazel eyes gleaming the reflection of scattered leaves. A ray of light traced the carving I love you R.B on the bench. She mouthed Vincent's name. The second part was too muffled. I studied her lips.

"You once loved me as Rose Brown," she said.

She was the real Ruby Brooks, the one I invented, but not a fly-by-night puppy love. She was my sage. A tree full of wondrous multi-colored leaves within her eyes. Even the man-made penny bellied in the earth shared the coppery sun's radiance.

Rose's gaze no longer unsettled, for it wasn't my widow's peak, my inadequacy, nor this nefarious liquid undertow that morphed my perfectly comfortable pants into the lifeless wet corduroys that she was concerned with but maybe to preserve a little of her youth. I leaned over as Rose kept her head down nestling her hands on her lap. I groped for her quivering hand.

Holding her hand couldn't bring back her husband, but I held it till she felt warm.

We grinned at the few stubborn green leaves clinging to the knobby branches – they couldn't compare with the Technicolor soup, even the cruddy ones caked to my sneakers. The lazy sun poked its bulbous head from behind the trees, for the day's last hurrah. Beauty was the aging process itself.

Soaking each other in, our eyes met. I'd completely forgotten about her raucous cheering during those thumb-wrestling matches. I wanted to

John Gorman

ask Rose more about her life and questions about the great voyage of life in general. I sat quietly instead. We held hands following drifters and fluttering leaves.

132

Luz Strikes Again

Later that day I realized why Rose was so hung up on Helen's haircut. The Village Voice had the answer buried on page nineteen; apparently they weren't as swayed as most of the other rags. Had I picked up the Post or the Daily News first I would've known from the get-go.

Luz did it again, what seemed a million to one shot the first time became Déjà vu, but in her world anything, I suppose, was possible. She met Bubba Carlson a second time, in two weeks. According to this article, she'd been waiting in line with thousands of other people to have the Big Ham [as the media often referred to him] sign his freshly scripted, hot off the press, autobiography. Luz hadn't bought hers yet, but made it to the store long before the line was impossible to latch onto. From way out there you couldn't even be sure if Bubba Boy was inside yet, except that those nuts outside haggled whoever came out just to be sure the signing was still on.

She was in impeccable form and Bubba Boy wore a dumfounded grin, a guilty celeb caught by the flashbulb of a tyro paparazzo. Not having been there, I was a little uncertain how the story unraveled. I cross referenced as many periodicals I could get my hands on and knit together, what I presumed the story was apart from all the spin. Had she told me herself I'm not sure I could've sat still. She'd always criticized me for not paying the kind of attention she demanded. So what if I made a sudden twitch or turned to look away from her. I've never been the cool dude, not by a long shot, but sometimes, I took jackass advice like feigning boredom to seem more desirable.

I smiled to myself because I truly wished the best for Luz. I wished I could be like her. Can you imagine going up to the former president and telling him you've got something for him? Secret service men could judo flip you for making too much eye contact.

While all the chaos was unfurling in the bookstore, Luz seized an opportunity to slip her resume from her backpack into her newly purchased book. She hustled. Nobody accounted for the inimitable craftiness of Luz. The resume, a simple sheet folded over by the last page of a doorstopper of an autobiography hid her scheme. She didn't cause any trouble for the staffers when she handed over her backpack, so they let their guard down.

Do you remember me we met at Copacabana she told Bubba. He winced for a second, but then extended his hand, of course at Nydia

Valesquez's birthday party. Luz didn't miss the opportunity to mention that it had been her birthday as well. Bubba smiled at her, dropped the pen that he'd been using to sign all those autographs and placed his free hand atop hers so that now he was sandwiching hers from top to bottom.

Up to that point, the line had been moving rather quickly, book, sign, book, sign, so when the charming Luz, held things up by chatting with the former president, in a somewhat intimate way, it caused a scene. A photographer who noticed this began snapping shots. Carlson's eyes squished together the way they might, biting into a sour apple. Before he could open them, Luz had leafed through the book to whisk out the resume.

This is for you she told him. That's when the secret service men walled around the former president. There was no telling what might be inside that book, anthrax, a box cutter, a paper-thin bomb, a picture of their lovechild. They huddled closer, the way you might expect in a soccer match when the defending team is preparing for a penalty kick. Then one of them snagged the book, Luz's resume swished onto the table. She pressed it into shape.

Take this, I'd really love to work for you. Maybe we could practice your mambo you were a little shaky the last time. Don't worry, I'll get you wiggling suavecito. Just remember to keep both knees bent and your back straight. Break on one and keep the tempo, bop, bop, bah.

The secret service men shot each other quizzical glances. The moderator of the book signing smirked and people on the line began chattering to one another while Luz busted into mambo mode.

Twice in two weeks, could anybody be that lucky? Well, she was and I didn't believe it, I mean who would believe that kind of story, the first time around – you just don't meet people who dance with celebrities the way people used to way back whenever.

Even the Wall Street Journal had a slice about it. Suddenly, it made sense to me, Rose's concern for Helen. There was a connection between her and her husband, Vincent, who'd run out on her. Of course Bubba didn't walk out on Helen, but you couldn't help wonder what the former first lady must have been thinking about seeing Luz sparkle in her husband's eyes. And Rose wanted to see if the former First Lady's stain of rejection matched her own.

I, on the other hand, was just happy to know Luz was still in town. Knowing that she was still around made things a little better, after all I might get lucky and see her again before I shipped off to France.

A Box Marked Perishables

I dipped into the fridge and debated about what scabby fruits to skin. The plums were between prunes and mothballs so I opted for a stony chunk of bread and olives. Spitting out olive pits disgusted me. I balled them into the napkin so I didn't have to see the yuck.

After my snack, I went into Luz's room to be closer to her things. To find clues about the things she wouldn't tell me. I marveled at the picture of her coupled with President Carlson. Some jeans and tops coiled into a mannequin on her bed just as she left them. I pulled the comforter over the clothes as if tucking Luz in. When I grew tired of that, I ironed some of her tops.

With the lights out and rumbling steam pipes keeping me awake, I went onto the fire escape the way I did waiting for Luz to come home. The traffic lights flickered a hollow glow onto the ashen streets whether or not anybody crossed. I still wanted her and couldn't settle for the dream. I'd felt a greater loss since I'd admitted to Rose my crush on Luz. Why did I have to bump into Rose and spill my guts? Opening up to her, I revealed more to myself. It made me uneasy. The more I dwelled on it I came to realize I had this need to share. I needed to prove to Luz that living together could be complimentary. It wasn't a crutch, but I think she had to see if I could handle being on my own. This must have mattered to me since I was an only child. I wasn't trying to hog her space. She treated the apartment as a hostel. What worried me though was the confluence of wanting to make her both happy and proud. That's the way a son might act, not a lover. If that's what it boiled down to, I wasn't going to waste Luz's time. I needed the chance to deliberate.

The more I considered us, the more I realized how we consummated nothing but flesh. Sometimes it felt so real, her skin, naked against mine with nobody else in the world, a magical spirit unleashed, buoyant, wriggling from our collective consciousness, rising beyond us. We were so alive then, that magnetic undertow I'd felt when I first laid eyes on her while she was poking through my stuffed animals, we were connected by curiosity and I saw it in her eyes, until she let go.

Whatever was etched in my brain may have been pure fantasy like those nebulous childhood memories that I believed to be indubitably true, because I had heard them being true, because my folks or my aunts, uncles and cousins remembered them to be so.

I took a long hot shower with steam thick enough to build clouds. Sweat poured off my chin. I showered in water hot enough to cook chickens, as Luz would say.

I lay in Luz's bed. The blanket smelled of her and I could almost see teeth marks, clenches she'd made during bad dreams. Her pillow was a billowy cloud and light flittered in from the shades. I sifted for traces of her hair as songs from my youth peppered my thoughts. I pictured Luz popping up from out of nowhere just like that classic video where the sketch comes to life and dances before the love struck boy.

Luz was that sketch, too ethereal to grasp. I rustled in her bed, with wind winnowing through the cracked pane.

A pair of ballet slippers poked out from a box marked **P e r i s h a b l e** underneath the bed. The half-knotted laces fell over the side. The shoes glistened with new sheen. Luz had been a dancer for many years, but said nothing about taking classes even though I suggested she take some. Why should she waste her talent in a city filled with dance schools, hopefuls dreaming of big breaks? I took to heart her suggestions whereas she brushed mine off. She considered me too critical if I said give it a whirl. "Don't rush me. There's time," Luz would say.

"There really isn't," I told her. "You have to strike while the iron is hot. I'm not being critical. Take it from me, I know because I'm the king of pushing things off. You'll only regret it later on."

"I'm not old," Luz said. "Is that what you're insinuating?"

In that case, the iron stung me. When you cross the point, it's full steam ahead. My fault was letting it slide. A better friend would've been relentless the way she was with me. I wanted to reciprocate.

The box was crammed with junk: old newspapers, a broken umbrella, an Italian dictionary whose cover appeared to have been chewed off, perhaps by one of her doggy pals. Beneath a wrinkled apron was a thick envelope wound in bakery string. Inside the envelope were layers of bubble wrap that I set atop the box. I flipped through the pictures of what I presumed was Luz's hometown. There she was blowing out candles on a cake with her family surrounding her and I suppose it may have been her brother or a close friend, trying to push her head into the cake.

There were some of her lying in a bikini on milky-white sand, perhaps Acapulco. There was one of a handsome couple, which must have been her parents, her father garbed in a soccer jersey making a muscle so his biceps flexed and her mother holding his muscle, her brows crinkled as if to say, "That's all." They stood before a humble, but cozy, chalk-dusted house, Spanish-tiled roof, with a drooping wire dangling shirts and pants hung to dry just above their heads.

Family glimmered in their eyes. How did they appear so happy? And why would Luz keep this from me?

I remembered nights when she broke into Spanish and I realized she was talking on the phone to her family. According to what she had told me, they lived most of their life in a small town below Guadalajara, but she had relatives scattered throughout other pockets of Mexico. Her nephew, who wanted to be a world traveler just like her, had won many science competitions and his younger brother played soccer on the Junior Guadalajara team. This she let me know.

Whenever she peeled another layer, a great sparkle gleamed in her eyes, an unparalleled rosiness rouged her cheeks. It was a pleasure seeing her happy. She held back afterwards. I had to watch my step and not seem so eager to know more.

"You're not going to get weird on me?" she once said.

"Depends on your definition?" I said.

"Look, I don't mind if you come to visit," she said. "They'd probably like you, my nephews especially. But we're not adopting right now."

"What's that supposed to mean?"

"Let's just leave things the way they are."

Her last word, not mine, but I played her game.

No pictures of former lovers in the box though I'd expected a few. This made me feel a bit relieved. Not that such pictures didn't exist, but at least I hadn't seen them. There was another of her father holding a stick, a skinny mutt suspended by its teeth. In the background, some little boys squirted water pistols behind her father's back.

Then there was a peculiar one with her father's arm wrapped around a woman's waist that looked like my mother. The similarity was alarming. Her hair was bleached. Scantily clad in bikini top and bottom with only a trace of pink lipstick, her hands rummaging through his choppy hair. His arms clutched her the way a lifeguard rescues somebody drowning.

For a good while, I studied the picture until I was certain it was my mother.

What the hell was this doing in Luz's box marked perishables?

For the rest of the day, I rattled my brain trying to figure a plausible explanation for all of this, but nothing made any sense. I knew my mother had been to Mexico. She was fond of mentioning a man named Juan Carlos who she'd wanted to marry. Every once in a while his name crept up as if I'd met him and she was waiting for me to ask what was new with him.

Had I found this picture tucked away at my parents' place things would have made better sense. This was bizarre.

137

Home Sweet Home

The next morning I woke to my parents arguing. They never stocked decent coffee in the house just instant so their little brouhaha was the perfect brew to get going. I tossed my old sailboat-knit quilt onto the floor then slid off the pullout. My life had become a tumble from one pullout couch to another. Why should Thanksgiving be any different?

It felt odd being in the old stead, but I wasn't completely shocked like the time I woke up with my buddy Thomas on Jones Beach and our sneakers were gone, right off our feet, socks included. It felt odd because I thought I'd completely washed away that homesick feeling and it seemed perhaps I hadn't. Not entirely.

It was nice, in a masochistic sort of way that they had enough passion to argue with such vigor. Nowadays people could care less about their mates. Dad had probably ruffled some papers or knocked over the mug of change he kept on the table nearest their bed.

I was entitled to eavesdrop, kissing my ear to the wall. I didn't need to see them and yet I knew exactly how they were posed. Mom's gruff voice, pleading for a coffee, cursed blue notes – oh the memories. The first time I'd heard my mother crank her way into a morning – twenty odd years ago – it was quite a shock because she looked like my mother, but didn't sound like her. I wondered if all adults had this dual personality. Without coffee, and a warm bath, she was unbearable, like Luz.

In any event, I imagined my mother uncoiling from the blankets, pursed and ready to lash into action. This I knew by the way the bed was squeaking. She rocked herself on the edge when building up her anger, the way a pitcher might practice the windup.

"Listen to me you creep, you are not, I repeat not giving his stuff away," Mom said.

"He told me to get rid of the books," Dad replied.

"You're not touching anything," Mom said.

Though the wall obstructed my view I heard Mom's teeth grinding.

"I need more room to put my papers."

"Try the recycling bin."

"Ask him if you don't believe me, he said I could put my stuff in his old bookcase?" Dad said.

"I didn't see you talking with him last night. Don't pull this phony baloney on me."

"We can't keep it all forever. He doesn't even live here anymore."

"Make sure your desk is cleared off before the guests arrive."

"Aye, aye, Captain."

"Go ahead, waste another day at the homeless shelter and let me do all the cleaning again."

"Get Benny off his ass. It's about time he pitches in."

"He's tired."

"Well, no wonder. He was out all night. Look, I'll get out of your hair. Just give me the box and I'll be on my merry way."

"It's staying put," Mom said.

I knew she was clamping her ankles around the box and Dad struggling to snag it from her. She usually kept things low on account of Dad's bad back, that way he'd give up before having to make an appointment with his chiropractor.

"These are poor kids who've got nothing," Dad said. "Don't you know what today is?"

I pressed my ear closer. The wall was cold so I peeled off my pillowcase and spread it to blanket my ear.

"It's the right thing to do," Dad continued, "What time are we going to eat?"

"The same time we eat every year, not that your memory is getting any better."

"Look Trudy, I'm not going to argue. I've got to run, at least give me that autographed ball?"

"Make a move and I'll bean it off your head."

"Have it your way."

Drawers slammed. Galumphing footsteps followed. I made a quick break for the bathroom down the end of the hall, but as I got within a few steps of the bathroom I heard Dad groan.

"Benny, can you wait a second? I'm in a rush."

"It'll take you at least five and a half seconds to get over here."

Dad walked briskly. As he approached me I held the door wide open for him, palm outstretched. He patted my open hand.

"You call that a tip."

He shut the door. So I decided to get a bowl of cereal since when the Thanksgiving preparation got under way God help you if you were loitering in the kitchen.

Just before I had the chance to make it safely across the hall I heard Mom's shrilly voice.

"Did you find the cufflinks, Benny? Don't pretend I don't know you're out there. I hear you creeping about."

"Not yet."

"They're not in your closet, I looked two days ago. They might be –"

Dad's heavy steps echoed down the hall.

"Did you open the window in there?" she said.

"It's thirty degrees outside," Dad said, toweling off his face.

"It better not stink when I get in there."

I searched for the old fire engine cufflinks Aunt Belinda gave me many moons ago, and every year she was just as shocked to learn that she was the one who bought them. Matching different ties to my white dress shirt, I examined my gaunt neck in the mirror. The paisley tie was too bottom heavy and the blue and red rep tie was too Princeton or Dartmouth. I didn't want to burst any bubbles. Aunt Belinda might not send any more checks. Not that I should have been thinking in my old way, but if I could make off with a little something I'd be in better shape for my trip.

There were a couple of straggly hairs on my neck, stubble peppering my cheeks. It was inevitable. I was going to have to shave. Holiday shaving was more exasperating than work shaving, because at least with work I could rationalize the chore, but for the family it seemed a complete waste of effort. If I didn't do it I wouldn't hear the end of it plus I'd get a bunch of razors as stocking stuffers for Christmas.

I bit the bullet thereby derailing my system which meant greater fuzziness for the ensuing week.

Mom barged into the room catching me by the mirror in my white shirt, bottomless except for my baby blue boxers. She inspected them to see if they were clean.

"You could knock," I said. "I'm in my underwear."

"That shirt's not ironed. Let me see." She examined it up close. "Is that the one with the – there's a spot."

"My cufflinks will hide it."

"You should wear one of your father's shirts. I'll bring one."

"NO. Look, this one's fine. I'll roll up the sleeves if I can't find the cufflinks."

I started to.

"You're not going to dress like a vacuum cleaner salesman. I'll bring in his blue and white. You look handsome in stripes."

"I don't want his shirts."

"One shirt."

"I don't want any of his shirts."

"How about the black ribbed turtleneck, I've always thought it makes you look very mature."

"No."

There were many gray turtlenecks in his closet. She would drag them all out if she had to. Appearance mattered most.

"His neckline is too big for me. Do you want me to look like a clown?"

"Then I'll iron your shirt."

"If I can have some peace. You'll iron my pants as well."

I took off my shirt and handed it to her. She checked me over as if she was a doctor examining an undernourished child from a third world country. I walked back to the dresser.

"Did you finish the thank you note to Aunt Belinda?"

"Wheels are in motion."

"You have to write her a quick note. I'll bring some stationary."

She had that funny twinkle in her eyes.

"What are you thinking?" I said.

"You write the note and I'll just trim it a bit," Mom said teasing a few of my stray hairs.

"No way."

"Come on, you've got some straggly ends. It won't take long."

"Don't you dare. Get away from my tail."

"I promise I won't make it too short."

"That's what you said last time."

"Everybody used to love the way I did your hair as a child."

"You put a bowl over my head."

"You look handsome when people can see your face."

She darted out, keeping the door wide open, not allowing me a rebuttal. I continued my search for the old-fashioned fire engine cufflinks. I alternated wearing them either for Thanksgiving or Christmas, but only once a year. For some reason if they couldn't be found there would be a massive hex on our holiday. As if one already hadn't surfaced.

Fumbling through my old dresser, I found a bunch of old socks, unused handkerchiefs, the blue and yellow, hand-knit mittens my mother made for me years ago stuck together by a piece of gum or maybe something else; I picked at it. The plush cotton made my fingers warm. Matchbox cars and other misplaced trinkets cluttered that supposedly "sock and accessory drawer." We had a very loose definition of what fit into the category accessories, including virtually everything and excluding almost nothing. There was a pair of tickets for "Starlight Express", which incidentally was my third Broadway Show. Every year Mom took me to see a new Broadway Show, it was her ill-attempt to squish culture into me, albeit kitschy, but culture nonetheless. Mom gave me a choice that year to either see that or the "King and I" which happened to be the last time Yul Brenner ever performed. I'm not sure why she put the decision in my hands considering she usually did things her way, but I was really ticked off for the whole performance. It must have been the dumbest show ever. It made no sense, it was just a stupid roller derby on a stage. I remembered hoping the cast would flop over on their heads when they took their final bow.

***

Whips of light spilled in from the window sweeping over the dusty floor as I wrestled with the curtain. We had an hour left to get everything shipshape before guests arrived. The turkey was still basting in the oven and there were plenty of snacks for Aunt Belinda to munch on when she naturally arrived ahead of schedule to boss us around before the get together officially got under way.

Over by our family photo collaborative, I couldn't help but imagine that picture of Mom with Luz's father. Its image became the centerpiece transmogrifying the family lineage.

Instead of my great, great grandfather Eugene Fluke the Confederate who was supposed to have rescued General Stonewall Jackson from a ditch he'd fallen into festered with poison oak, nursing the General back to health, becoming the South's most highly decorated nurse slash infantryman – there was a picture of a dark man with a Pueblan poncho. Instead of batting baseballs, my cousins bounced soccer balls. The Female Flukes smiles improved one-hundredfold with longer, sexier hair, devoid of the pastiness that many of my white bread family members personified. Still, it was unsettling having our family blotted out.

My image faded then returned. It occurred to me that I was having a problem processing the different pictures of me growing up as if I was hoping I could keep each individual image preserved from their respective moments in time. I remembered back when I thought I was being clipped out of the family because I'd seen Mom snipping pictures. I tried so hard to remember the images to keep from being expunged from the family record. No matter how hard I tried recalling my youth I couldn't preserve it. Some way or another you slide out of your sweet memories – life startles that way.

Why did I have to go back to her room? This was the punishment for being a peeping tom. My whole life a great big vacuous bag of what ifs had broken, and out came this image, like a microscopic lens. All I needed to do was look at it carefully. My head pounded seeing my mother in her own, unbridled life.

Out Of The Blue, Luz's Favorite Shade

Luz called later that morning, on my parent's phone. It was definitely her voice on the other line. It went dead for a good ten seconds. I was sure I'd lost her and then she came back, fuzzy, but there while I was fumbling with a new bag to go around the garbage basket waiting for Luz to speak.

"I've decided to meet your folks," she said, "If that's fine by you."

"Sure, no problem," I said, realizing that the bag didn't belong in the sink.

"So you just need to give me the directions and I'll come on by. Does your mom prefer milk or dark chocolate?"

"Anything with nuts."

When I hung up, I still had a million things to do before everybody arrived.

I was useless around the house under normal circumstances, but with Luz resurfacing, I couldn't think straight. Mom sent me out to pick up some last minute bottles of seltzer and prune juice for Aunt Chloe. When the festivities got under way, there was no telling how embarrassing it could get for me. Luz was going to be in for a rude awakening. Our gatherings bordered on surreal. Booze and stupidity afflict all families, but affected mine tremendously. A special calculus was needed to quantify its effects on me. During major holidays, scrapbooks, baby booties, my first jockstrap – anything – could pop out. My dad whipped that jockstrap out of the old bat bag one time. One by one the whole family, a bunch of self-ordained garment inspectors, handled my sacred equipment while my face reddened.

Perhaps I'm painting the wrong picture. I was mainly scared of Luz finally seeing, for herself, how nauseating my parents' admiration was for me. No woman wants to duke it out with a doting mother. And I didn't want to referee, not in that Freudian-style tug-of-war between mother and significant other.

Luz would see for herself why I was the way I was. Other children went through those stages complaining that their parents didn't understand them or that they were fascists who wouldn't allow them to express themselves, I, on the other hand, had those kind of parents who thought that whatever I did was wonderful.

Now, I'm not saying they were cool with stinko grades or a disrespectful, potty-mouthed twerp, not every day at least. Yes, they wanted me to apply myself, but it was alright for me to do it at my pace and if I needed Mom to pen a book report that's how it had to be.

Only recently, my dad wanted me to get off my hump and take some kind of government job that he was forever mailing me applications regarding.

Don't get me wrong, my mother had plenty of suggestions of her own for me; to become an ambassador because I was the designated diplomat of the family; or an oceanographer, because she remembers back when I was five, I fastened a plastic fire extinguisher onto my back and put on my dad's old ski goggles and took baths as if I was Jacques Cousteau.

From what I told Luz about my dad she already liked him. She told me she saw him waltzing happy-go-lucky through life with a grin, never caring what others thought of him. Was at peace with himself, the complete opposite of me. She was right on the money, that I had once been close with him. We'd only really drifted apart when I grew too big to take trips out to the ball field with him. We'd spend hours there. He'd pitch hundreds of balls at me and I'd swat them deep into the outfield. We usually arrived early with the joggers and Tai Chi enthusiasts. Gulls swirled through the sky and I swung with all my might trying not to hit them but reach their height. We never played on fenced-in fields, always in wide-open spaces.

These were the most memorable times I shared with my dad. I admitted to Luz how my mother and I both had begun to treat him like a guest in his own home.

I still caught him appraising my trophies in his den, and I watched him admiring the glittering plastic junk as if they were rare birds. Why would parents be happy with such mediocre achievements? It made me angry. And although I didn't see this when I was a stupid kid I picked fights with them, but especially with my dad, letting him know firsthand that I sucked. He, of course, vigilantly defended me as if he stood to win a million-dollar-settlement. He crowned me the Batting King. He turned a blind eye as I fudged my stats, erasing over and then rerecording hits into the scorecard.

Was I so hard up for a pat on the back that I needed this kind of constant adulation? Just before I was ready to leave the game, I was starting to realize my place in a society of modern day gladiators. I wasn't willing to lift my sword anymore, not if I already knew I couldn't claim my own kingdom.

This was too hard to take, for everybody, so naturally I nodded my head whenever my folks made suggestions. Whatever I did was fine by them. In private, they devised ways to be good cop bad cop so that I might come to my senses. In an ideal world, I could do anything I pleased, but I wasn't a dope, I knew how much faith they had in me. Things may have been different had I not mentioned my bid at street entrepreneurship.

That's when Dad blitzed me with city job applications. Mom told me to yes him; she bribed me with my old room and an endless supply of pork chop dinners if I'd finish my Masters. Did she think I forgot the torture she put me through in Little League when she made me wear a batting helmet in the outfield because she was afraid I'd get hurt? I still hadn't forgiven my dad for letting her get away with that crap, but either one of them could be beyond annoying if they suspected I was suffering in any way.

I gulped a deep breath. Luz would see everything. It was bad enough losing her, but then to have her come over and see this spectacle. She'd laugh herself silly and leave me with a lingering humiliation. I was twenty-nine, but I was still a careless child watching his balloon sail away with the wind.

We tended to our tasks, Mom fixing a tray of celery and carrot sticks escorted by a plate of white goop and I tried not to upend her with the vacuum cord. She hopped over it as though it was a jump rope and I wormed underneath the sofa swallowing whatever lurked in that nebulous zone.

This dutiful harmony was our paragon of communication, what my dad was never quite able to master with her. Under these circumstances, with the impending guests moments from waltzing in, there was no time for questions, only decisions.

We had almost come to the point where I didn't have anything to say and that hurt, because when I wasn't with her there were lots of things I wanted to say. This seems absurd but I had become so stingy with my time that I hated repeating myself. Now, it wasn't that so many great things were going on in my life, besides the fact I was finally growing into an adult.

There was only that question of my mother's past by some paradox of space time continuum that worried me, that could somehow, through some extraterrestrial's primary school science project, redirect my inertia so that I would either split into a fractionalized being or be permanently blotted out of existence.

I felt like hired help while folding the napkins on the dining table.

***

When I greeted Luz, picking her up from the train station, she shoved a bouquet of flowers in my face. She was dressed to kill in a full-length suede coat with the belt left untucked. Beneath the coat, she wore the Merino wool top that I'd seen, on occasion, draped over the chair by the kitchen, reeking of cigarettes, even though she stuck to the same story that she never took a puff.

She went on and told me she had a dream about sitting on my mother's lap.

"I was just a child plucking at a flower," she said, "I think it was a violet, pulling apart one petal at a time. You know, he loves me, he loves me not, that bit. But it was so much more innocent."

"Let me get this straight," I said, juggling the packages so that the flowers flopped over to give me an unobstructed view of her face, "You were sitting on my mother's lap."

"That's right."

"How do you know it was her?"

"I just know."

"But you never met her."

"She was braiding my hair. Kind of the way mine is now. It sort of tickled and I giggled and then she sort of giggled as well, the two of us carrying on like sisters."

"Where was I when all of this was going on?"

"I'm not sure really," she said, smoothing out the ribbon on the box.

"Was I out buying milk or dental floss?"

"No, actually I don't think you were part of this dreamscape."

"I don't believe it."

"What do you think it means?" she said, borrowing my finger to rewrap the bow.

"Nothing. People have dreams like that all the time."

"You've dreamt of my mother?"

"Well, no."

"Then how can you say people have dreams like that all the time."

"It's just the way we're made up. We can't account for the wandering mind, sleeping or subconscious."

I was mad at myself for letting another opportunity slip away, especially since this was such a natural transition.

"You know we could've come together," she said, squinting trying to discover some new clue about me.

"Yeah, well if I knew where you were that might have helped."

"What is it about your face that seems so different? I can't put my finger on it."

Luz ran her fingers atop a hedge as we cut through Greenway South. We stopped for a moment so I could show her where I had once wrestled with my friends and climbed trees.

"You must have been such a cute little boy. Oh, my gosh, I don't believe it. You cut your hair! "

I reached around the back hoping my tail had grown back, it had been there so long it was kind of like losing a limb.

"What made you do it?"

"I lost a bet."

Forgive and Forget Me Not

We stopped a few blocks from my parent's house by Flagpole Park where I used to climb trees and dig for ants when I was a kid. The old flagpole, rusted to the core, lay on its belly atop rough-hewn grassy patches and caked dirt. It looked more like the shell of a once vibrant torpedo. Not that I'd ever seen one of those. The pole's sharp point gave me this impression.

Somewhere in the park, probably under the flagpole, were the Matchbox cars I buried. I'd once been enamored with the idea of unearthing hidden treasures and had let weeks go by before excavating my cars. It took no time to hide them, but seemed almost impossible to dig them up. I wasn't sure what was worse, not being able to find them or if some other pirate had beaten me to my bounty.

From my vantage point, a large hole filled the powder blue sky where the star spangled banner of my youth once fluttered.

***

"What the heck did you do to your hair?" Luz said.

"I lost a bet," I said.

"What bet?"

"No bet. My mom cut it."

"It's not you. I mean, it is, but no, just not you."

"Forget my hair, what are you doing here?" I asked.

"Benny, I'm really sorry I left so abruptly. These past few weeks have been brutal."

"Well, it hasn't been a picnic for me, either."

"I'd take it back if I could," Luz said, startled so it seemed by the frankness of her words. She scraped the tip of her shoe in the dirt as if erasing melancholy and I hoped she'd say more. The sun slipped through the trees beaming off our bodies throwing off gossamer-fine shadows. Luz didn't quite seem Luz, but an unbridled ideal. The blanching brightness made me see blue grains of dust and then the outlines of a sculpture. Yes, that's what Luz appeared to me as an ebullient sculpture. How odd, how out of place there in the park I'd lost so many toys from my childhood.

I couldn't hold back anymore. Maybe it had something to do with not being able to see her so clearly at that moment, but I let it gush.

"I wake up in the middle of the night, if I'm not already up, wondering, worrying, watching for you out on the fire escape hoping you'll make your way up the block."

"You probably hate me," Luz said.

"I should. Look, I know you think sleeping together was a mistake. I'm a creep for nosing into your room. And the whole thing with your niece's doll –"

"I'm over it."

"I'm not."

"That's not what I mean, not us anyway."

I moved to the side. I really preferred not seeing Luz so clearly, but the sun was making me woozy.

"I can't go on pretending," I said. "Luz, I want to be with you."

"You'll probably want to dump me after I tell you."

"Tell me what?"

She pulled some letters out from her shoulder bag, a big heap of weathered letters wrapped in rubber bands. A couple of the rubber bands had split, but were retied, double-knotted at the ends and looked like party favors or baby squid tentacles.

"There's no good way to start," Luz said, sitting on the concrete base to the old memorial.

"What's this?" I said struggling to read from upside down. I crouched to get to her level.

"These letters are from your mom," Luz said.

"What are you doing with them?" I asked.

"I figured it out when I saw that picture of your mom at our place. My Papa had kept some pictures of her. They wrote each other for ten years."

"What the hell is going on here?" I said grabbing Luz by her shoulders.

It became quite clear to me seeing Juan Carlos's name scripted in the blue ballpoint ink. Who else could it have been, but the same Juan Carlos whose name I'd heard so often peppered in and out of conversations Mom had been so glib in sharing. The squiggly-handed penmanship gave the allusion of rippling waves. A blue smudge above the J made me think of a fresh bruise purpling under a harsh glow of light. Seeing this in Mom's handwriting stunned me in a way his name said aloud never had.

Sorting through the stack, I noticed the letters were made out to Mom's maiden name and addressed to Jackson Heights where she had lived before she was married.

"My papa was already married to my mother when he sent them."

"That can't be."

I stood up and dug both fists into my pockets feeling the weight of my worries deep into the soles of my shoes. One of my laces was undone, but I didn't bother tying it.

"I should hate your mom. For a long time I did. But I can't let it eat me. I loved my papa. Don't you dare judge him!"

"I haven't said a word."

"My mom tried to keep him happy. 'Eyes that don't see, hearts that don't feel,' she used to say. The words go on. The affair may have died, but the feelings burn. Papa had kept the letters all those years. I found them stuffed in an old cigar box cleaning out his closet after he passed away. As a kid, I used to snoop in his closet to be closer to his things having his shirts' warm cloth sleeves brush against my cheek. They smelled of him. I hated when they were freshly pressed because then the fabric lost a little bit of him. Imagine, all those years he hid the letters. What if I discovered those letters as a kid?"

I thought back to my childhood when I'd seen Mom clipping photos from the family album. The fear of being snipped away myself, as dingbatty as it was, sharpened my senses. It made me who I am.

I took a long look at Luz, at this bundle of bricks she dumped that she'd been shouldering for so long. We shared an improbable kismet. Still, I couldn't shake the thought of her rejecting me.

"Benny, don't hate me. But I have to talk with your mom. The time has come."

"Not if you can't find the house," I said.

"I have the address," Luz said. "I took it from a letter in your room, before I left. I even rang your parent's bell. I chickened out though. I ran so fast right out of my shoe. I didn't care. Then I hobbled off without looking back. I took the subway home in my stocking feet."

"Why all the sudden now?" I said. "On Thanksgiving, for crying out loud."

"Call me crazy, but I want to see your family dynamics. You've made them into this nutty circus. I'm going to cut down the tent. I think you're making most of it up, no matter. I want to see you with your family."

"I never brought anybody over, never for a holiday."

Luz took my hand.

Knowing all that I knew should have frightened me, should have made me want to run for cover, but there in Luz's warm, sympathetic hand I felt snug like a blanket tucked up to my chin. She puffed a billowing wreath of breath from her soft, pink lips. I didn't want to let go.

All In The Family

Guests are synonymous with pests in our household, I warned Luz as I sat her in the living room. She didn't believe me. I was a bit nervous. I had no idea what my mother would think of her and vice versa. It was only a matter of time before Luz made the revelation. The inevitability didn't faze me it was the element of surprise that had me worried. My whole family was over and I'd never had a date for the big turkey day, not ever.

"Look, if you're not comfortable, you can split," I said.

"I've made up my mind," Luz said inches from my lips.

Aunt Chloe poked her head out from the kitchen. My heart skipped, but I stayed close to Luz trembling with the desperate urge to kiss her. I got the sense she needed to reconcile this matter with my mother before we could go any further.

Aunt Chloe, stalwart busybody, expert napkin-folder, looked on and made me feel as if she caught me doing something naughty. And maybe she did because I was bottling up my feelings again. I thought of what Luz said that ships must be bottled inside me.

When Aunt Chloe's cuckoo head pulled back into the kitchen, I kissed Luz's cheek. She smelled of huckleberries. I went into the kitchen and watched Mom chopping raw carrots into the stuffing. I nabbed some celery bits resting on the serving platter. Aunt Chloe procured her own chopping board. She gave the appearance she was eager to help, but she didn't fool anybody, not even herself. We knew she came early because she was lonely. Chloe was Mom's youngest sister, but looked fifteen years older than both my mother and Aunt Belinda, primarily because she didn't touch up her graying hair or slight facial growth above her lip and she wore dresses that looked like hospital gowns. She was built like a shot-putter and had the most annoying, hollow laugh.

"You've done a great job with the kitchen," Aunt Chloe said, "Love the sunflower."

She raised her arm above her head, spreading her fingers outward, letting her arms drop slowly, the cascading effect mimicking the sunflower on the wall. She grabbed a piece of dark chocolate, since the box was unguarded atop the corner hutch. Gazing at it briefly before popping it in her mouth, she was probably wondering where the Baci was hidden, since Mom often hid her Baci from the chocoholic.

"They're just Russell Stover," Mom said, watching her.

"Well, they're tasty anyway," Aunt Chloe said, rushing over to the wall to feel its texture, then demonstrating her version of a sunflower again.

"I finished it two days ago," Mom said, "It changes the mood doesn't it? I can't tell if the room feels bigger or smaller but it just seems different. Benny, what do you think?"

"Lovely. Listen, my friend Luz is here, thought you'd want to know," I said.

"What? You never said you were inviting anybody. I'm not even dressed," Mom replied.

"Must be serious, huh Benny?" Aunt Chloe said.

I shrugged.

"Go ahead Trudy get dressed I'll lend a hand." Aunt Chloe dipped back into the box of candy.

"Shooosh, everybody out of here," Mom said, brushing us away as if swatting flies away from her cranberry sauce.

Mom peeled the bandana off her head, the matted one she wore solely for cooking or deep dish baking, tossed it onto the counter, then plodded into the living room for two seconds throwing out a casual hello.

Luz made me hold the flowers again then dipped into her bag and my mouth went agog when I saw the letters poking out. This time she only took out a lump of cornbread wrapped in cellophane.

"Get a grip will you," Luz said.

Mom charged past us straight for her room. She made a sidelong glance going up the stairs.

Luz appraised the pictures perched atop the dry sink that Mom had recently added a new coat of lilywhite paint.

"I just knew you were an adorable kid," she said pointing to a picture of me in this ridiculous captain's hat. I was eight at the time, the hat was so big it kept flopping off but it made such a cute shot that it needed to come out for family gatherings. Where it hibernated the rest of the year I couldn't say. Mom liked putting out new pictures every so often. She enjoyed testing her guests' detective acumen.

"You've seen one, you've seen them all," I said.

"Now, would he have said such sarcastic things," Luz said holding up the frame so that I was eye to eye with the little brat in the captain's hat. Nobody – not even Lost and Found – knew where he had vanished to.

We hardly had the chance to settle in before Mom snuck up on us.

"Benny, are you going to make a proper introduction?" Mom said snapping her necklace into place.

Luz eyed the tiny rubber creatures beaded around Mom's neck what were childhood toys of mine. Mom thought it shabby chic and received many compliments. When people asked of its provenience, she was only too happy to tell whomever that she made the necklace from her son's old toys. How clever? She'd launch into a dull story about me and then squeezed in her views on fashion, whatever suited her at the moment.

"This is Luz," I said.

"It's nice to meet you Mrs. Fluke," Luz said.

"I'm Trudy."

"Benny's talked so much about you I feel I know you already," Luz said.

I grimaced, but Luz paid no attention. She handed my mother the lump of cornbread. Mom passed me the cornbread as if it were a dead bulb or a spare part that needed removing.

"These are also from Luz," I said, handing off the flowers to Mom.

"You really didn't need to bring anything. Luz, that's a pretty name. Tell me, is it a nickname?"

"Yes, Lucia is my real name, but I can't remember anybody but my grandmother calling me that. I was named after my papa's mother, mi abuelita."

I relished this new puzzle piece for maybe ten seconds. My thoughts scrambled when the bell rang. We hadn't a chance to sit.

"Benny, get the door," Mom said.

"It's your house," I said.

"Don't be silly," Mom said. "Tell him Luz."

Luz looked over in deference toward my mother and I went to get the door. It was Aunt Belinda and Uncle Hank. Aunt Belinda draped in what looked like a Kodiak bear. She had the longest, fluffiest fur coat in the universe. She could fit a small family snugly inside it, a top-of-the line refrigerator, perhaps a Chippendale armoire. It was a furry monstrosity, unnecessary, but definitely warm. It suited her.

"You never thanked me for the check I sent you," Aunt Belinda said, shedding her coat.

"Gobble, gobble to you, too," I said collecting the unraveled goods.

"Don't kiss me, I have a bit of a cold," Aunt Belinda told my mother.

Uncle Hank took his cue and half-hugged Mom. I shook his hand.

"Go easy will you," Uncle Hank said, pretending I was crushing him.

I never particularly cared for my bulbous-headed uncle's smarmy routine. I forced a grin.

Dad snuck in a little while after. Mom hated him loitering around the house when she did her preparations. He meant well, but Mom needed things done just so or she would have a conniption. Plus, he better served the soup kitchen where he volunteered in Brooklyn. Dad raised the shopping bag with ginger ale and rye bread so that Mom would know he didn't forget. Mom liked to have a turkey sandwich when the guests left. She hardly ate a bite when everybody was over.

Dad smiled at Luz as if offering a sign of peace to a parishioner seated the pew behind him at church.

"He's just the delivery guy," I said.

Luz punched my arm.

"That's your father," she said. "You look just like him."

Luz went up to my dad. He shook her hand and had a dumb grin on his face like all the times I gave him goofy ties for Christmas. I could tell that he knew what she meant to me. A knot turned in my gut. The only thing I could think about was that Dad never shared the birds and the bees talk with me, and for that I was grateful.

There was hardly time to sloppily pour ourselves some cocktails before we were forced into the dining room. Mom planned gatherings this way. Get them in, get them out was the standard modus operandi. Pilgrim hats marked the boys' spots while the bonnet-shaped candles reserved the girls' places. Uncle Hank looked at the pillows spread out on the floor and whispered something to the old ball and chain. Aunt Chloe helped Mom bring in the platters. Luz asked to help but was denied the offer and was therefore relegated to the living room. As a consolation prize, Luz got to listen to Uncle Hank butcher songs from "South Pacific." Some Enchanted Evening. Not quite yet. She was a good sport though and also had to put up with my dad's religious nuttiness. She encouraged him by nodding and appeared to follow his talking points. Luz took Dad's obsidian-beaded rosary between her thumb and forefinger. She held the beads as if really saying "Hail Marys" then watched with great zeal as my dad pulled out a picture of Our Lady of Mount Carmel. He passed along a few card-sized Saints and before anybody could object, Dad was merrily flipping through his cards as if dealing a blackjack hand and, of course, he couldn't help himself when he reached the Virgin of Guadalupe. He told the same story over and over again, I believe, because it rang true for him.

"You know who that is?" Dad said to Luz, referring to the little man standing at the feet of the Virgin of Guadalupe.

"Juan Diego," Luz said.

"She's good," Dad said to nobody in particular then returned to the picture. "You know the story about him, when he opened up his tilma and the roses fell to the bishop's feet, the image of the Virgin of Guadalupe appeared."

"Dad, nobody wants to hear this," I said.

"Don't be so rude," Luz said, "Go ahead, I'm listening, Mr. Fluke."

Dad continued, "Well, Juan Diego was a humble man, a Mexican Indian. One day he came upon a young woman who he thought was an Aztec Princess. When he had a good look at her, he knew that she was the Virgin Mary. Her face beamed like an angel. She told him that she wanted a shrine built in her honor. Juan Diego promised, but when he told the Bishop that he'd seen the Blessed Mother with his own eyes the Bishop didn't believe him. He needed proof. The Virgin appeared again to Juan Diego, but this time she gave him a bundle of roses. Roses, you know, don't come from Mexico and when the Bishop saw them and the Virgin's impression marked on Juan Diego's tilma he was so amazed. He got on his knees and promised to build the shrine. Before I die, I have to visit the sacred place," Dad said.

"It's beautiful," Luz said.

"You've been there?" Dad asked with great zeal.

"It's not so far from where my family lives in Mexico."

Mom's ears perked up when she heard this.

"I love Mexico." Mom said. "I almost lived there. Have you been to Guanajuato?"

"No," Luz replied.

"They say you haven't been to Mexico unless you've been to Guanajuato. But you're from Mexico," Mom said.

"And when the sand gets into your shoes you keep going back," Luz said.

Mom had almost chimed in this last part save for Luz being a few beats ahead.

"Where in Mexico are you from?" Mom asked.

"Mexico City," Luz said.

"Yes, but it's a big city, where exactly?" Mom repeated.

"In a little part called Plaza Haragon. We have many markets and the best concha bread around. It's not far from the center."

"And the sweetest mangoes," Mom said.

"You've been to Plaza Haragon," Luz said, her voice almost cracking.

I was puzzled that Mom didn't mention Juan Carlos's name. She'd said it so casually whenever we broached the subject of Mexico you'd think he might even waltz into the room in time for coffee and cake.

Luz was growing uneasy. I think she relished the chance to listen to my dad pontificating. It must have put her mind at ease underneath all the stress pinching in around her. She twisted in Mom's direction every so often, but also remained attentive to my dad. Maybe it was simple manners, but I cherished her kind way and considered all the nonsense I put my dad through growing up, and the way I still acted selfish and uncaring.

"It's still dirty, though," Aunt Belinda two-cented. "What do they call that smog?"

Luz said the name, but I didn't catch it.

Mom got up from the table and headed to the corner hutch where she removed a brown and white plate.

"This is from Oaxaca. I've had it for years."

She let Luz pet the plate. Mom flipped it over to show the Oaxacan etching. Two finger-long cracks crosshatched the bottom. A bad glue-job patched it back together. It was a miracle Mom still had the plate after I accidentally shattered it while cruising the living room with my Big Wheels when I was four.

This year we ate tatami style, which might have made better sense last year since Mom had been waiting for her new flock of furniture to arrive. Instead, last Thanksgiving we dined at some long-forgotten inn tucked away in its Long Island nook. Mom prattled on about her find and that it saved her from doing dishes.

Though Dad tried to sit on the pillow he kept falling off, but Luz came to his rescue, propping him up, until he tossed the pillow aside, making as if he was dusting his hands off from the hassle. He and his new buddy chuckled.

After grace, manners went out the window. Plates filled with candied yams, creamy spinach, Luz's cornbread, and Cornish game hen and lumps of stuffing fashioned after wigwams, why I don't really know. In any event, I felt sorry for Luz that she had to eat with people that put tailgaters to shame. My aunts and uncles suggested our ancient hominid relatives, huddled around fresh kill in the savannahs of equatorial Africa.

I tapped Luz on the knee so she could catch Aunt Chloe, seated to the left of me, jabbering with a heaping mouthful. By glaring at the obvious, I wanted Luz to see that I wasn't embarrassed by the situation, but I was.

The room's glow dithered between flitting incandescent and cigar-bar dim. The hominids took turns lobbing disturbingly mundane questions about Mexico and one or two minor probes into Luz's family. After a while, Luz played a smaller part in the conversation. Mom and Aunt Belinda filled in for her espousing their respective romantic and sour impressions of Mexico. They talked lively and loudly being on opposite ends of the table. I've always thought of Thanksgiving as a cacophony of gab and grub. Maybe that summed up all our gatherings.

"I'm telling you, we stopped for breakfast in Sanbornes," Mom said. "I had Huevos Rancheros."

"And I'm telling you, I was as sick as a dog the first morning," Aunt Belinda insisted.

"You got sick at the end of the trip," Mom said.

"I know I was sick," Aunt Belinda said pointing with her fork. "I was hugging the toilet."

"And I was waiting for Juan Carlos to take me to the big soccer match," Mom said. She said it as easy as if offering another helping of stuffing. Luz's amber eyes gleamed, but I could see this whole situation frightened her.

I didn't do anything to calm her. My own worries smothered my caring side. The only sensible thing to do was to get it out into the open. It was right there anyway. Luz sat still. I wondered what she was thinking. Petty arguments we'd had paled in comparison to the emotional load hunched on her shoulders.

"Luz," I said, but her head was down.

Aunt Belinda grabbed my arm. She licked some gravy off her lower lip. The family prosecutor was ready to start an interrogation. After filling my chest with a generous huff, I exhaled trying to remember my excuse for not sending her stupid thank you note. Aunt Belinda shifted in her seat, munching on cornbread looking at me, through me. I imagined opaque things, to blunt her x-ray vision. At any given moment, questions would come darting at me, as well as food bits. She had the terrible habit of spraying food, drink, and gossip when she spoke.

"So what are you up to now?" she asked, pecking at the crumbs on her sleeve.

"Oh, you know, the usual. Previously, I was keeping track of the sharpest dart-slinging monkeys for this guy Mungo, but then he gave me the green light to be his prized thumb-wrestler. Here, you want to go a few rounds with me?" I said offering my hand.

"Can you believe this guy?" Aunt Belinda, said searching for affirmation. "When are you going to stop jerking around? You're not a kid anymore. You'll be thirty soon."

"But I look good for my age, don't I?"

"He really was quite a competitor," Luz trumped in. She basked in this diversion demonstrating with both thumbs. "You should have seen him. He even had his own cheering section."

"I don't know, Benny, you're crazy if you let this one go," Aunt Belinda said, then she leaned over me and added to Luz. "But you really shouldn't encourage him."

"That's what friends are for," I said in cheesy falsetto.

Luz crinkled her nose. She said nothing, but everything with her wet, glassy eyes. I wanted to take it back. She'd always been more than a friend even when it had all been wishing on my part.

The unsettling truth remained, where exactly did Luz and I fit in each other's lives? How could I be more to her without giving away part of myself? Intellectually, I grasped this even though my impulse shied away. Whenever I looked back into my youth, at times I came close to touching the nape of intimacy I pulled away because I didn't want to feel stupid about not knowing what to do next. It took me forever to make my first kiss simply because I didn't know where to put my hands. The echo of friends rang through my ears. It smacked of cowardice. It was a bitter lie.

"It's too bad Marcy couldn't come," I said to Aunt Belinda.

"Well, she's been so busy with work and you know how she took that extra long cruise last year. It's a shame but she'll be around for Christmas."

My cousin Marcy, the brightest bulb of the bunch, worked like a dog in Seattle or Portland, somewhere out in the Pacific Northwest, so she possessed, what you might consider, a permanent get-out-of-these-stupid-family-gatherings pass. With me having hyperactive genes for both guilt and weisenheimerness I could never truly break free. Unless, that is, I made the permanent cut.

Luz kept studying my mother. Every so often, she seemed on the verge of saying something. Pistons churned in her head. I tried distracting Luz to stop her staring, but eventually figured it pointless. What would I be thinking if the shoe was reversed? Could I, in good conscience, let Luz suffer any longer? Did I have some responsibility in this matter to make it easier on her, maybe by pulling Mom aside – I just didn't know how to break the news. I convinced myself that I didn't want to steal Luz's thunder. I got up and excused myself from the table. Luz looked my way as if I were abandoning her. I really didn't need to go to the bathroom, but I went anyway. I didn't bother with the one upstairs so I stepped into the one by the kitchen.

It was nice to have a moment of reprieve from the chaos of the day. Mom had a sailing motif going on in the downstairs' bathroom. She'd hung some sketches of classic sailboats, ones that had docked years ago by the South Street Seaport. A toy pirate ship of mine sat atop the wicker towel rack. The skull and bones pedant had been replaced by a plain blue flag that looked a heck of a lot like the toothpicks pinching the cheese cubes in the living room. Instead of washing my hands with the decorative soaps loafing on the ledge of the sink, I fished a bar of Ivory from the soap dish by the bathtub. I hated the cloying smell from decorative soaps.

It never occurred to me, but I think our bathroom was one of the few I'd been in that had zero reading material.

Too Hot In The Kitchen, Then Stay In The Bathroom

I was still in the bathroom when I heard chattering. I opened the door a crack so as not to be noticed. When I realized Luz was in the kitchen talking to my mother I stayed put. There was only one way out of the kitchen and if I made an exit, they'd see me. Luz clutched the well-worn pile of letters while Mom tended to the pies. Somehow it appeared a larger batch, another year's worth of cherished memories and unfulfilled promises sealed into musty envelopes. I have no idea what Luz was thinking, choosing this moment to make her revelation. Aunt Chloe could have snuck in to nibble on a chocolate turkey. I grew uneasy considering the contents of the letters, the consummated lust and longing. The whole while it was nearly impossible to stop thinking about Luz in my arms, the unbearable warmth of her skin wrapped around me and the gentle way she kissed me behind my ear.

"You startled me," Mom said as she turned.

"I'm sorry I didn't mean to," Luz said.

"Out, out of the kitchen," Mom said, "You're a guest."

"No, but you don't understand. I have something to show you."

"I have a rule of thumb. Nobody does dishes at my place and I don't do them at yours. Claro?"

"Claro," Luz said. She flicked at the rubber band binding the letters.

"What's that you've got there?" Mom asked.

"What if I showed you a piece of your past?" Luz said. "Would that be alright?"

Mom sprayed whipped cream onto the pumpkin pie. Some got on her fingers and she licked it off. She stopped, I imagine, to consider this fortune cookie question Luz posed.

"Did Benny put you up to this?" Mom said.

"No, he didn't."

"Then what on earth are you talking about?"

"I have a bunch of letters you wrote my papa. I've had them a long time."

"Your papa?" Mom said and dropped the can of whipped cream.

"I meant to come sooner. I just couldn't find the nerve."

Mom stared at the offering of letters. She wiped her hands on an oven mitt then reached for the letters but didn't take them. Instead, she leaned toward Luz.

"Oh my God, you're Juan Carlos's daughter."

"Yes."

They hugged making soft pats along each other's backs as if searching the dark for something lost; they touched hands but didn't link fingers. They waited for the other to speak then stumbled over the other's words. Luz broke the muddled stalemate.

"I discovered them going through his things on my last trip to Mexico. Papa died when I was in what you call high school, but we never got rid of all his stuff. When I stumbled upon the letters, I was very sad. But reading them I could see his joy. It confused and hurt me. I loved Papa and I told myself I had to know this piece of his past."

"I still have his letters," Mom said. "Then one day he stopped writing me. I don't know why but I had a strange, gnawing feeling he had died. Must have been ten years ago now, on a cold winter morning I had this sharp pain pounding in my head, creeping all the way down my spine. Then I imagined the soft touch of his hand on my cheek and the pain went away. A few days later I had this thick sense of loss."

"It was ten years ago," Luz said. "But he died in May."

Mom's face tightened. She tucked her lower lip and smoothed the ruffles of her skirt with her palms, then let out a deep sigh. Luz gave Mom a letter and my mother took it briefly. She licked her finger before taking the letter out of its envelope. She lulled there as if for a brief moment she was all by herself. She snapped out of her rumination perhaps she'd seen too much from her past, too quickly. She stuffed the letter back into the envelope and put it on the table.

She didn't appear to know what to do any more with her hands so she grabbed a plate and walked over to the sink. The choreography became awkward when only a moment ago they found it easy to hug while Mom embraced the memory of Juan Carlos. The hope that he was still alive faded from her cheeks. She absentmindedly turned on the tap, letting water rush into the sink. She didn't bother with her rubber gloves and squeezed the sponge into a ball. Luz went over to my mother and I stood by the bathroom door as if an intruder in my childhood home. Luz reached for the dish soap and poured a little into some bowls. Mom brushed the hair away from Luz's eyes. I felt both scared and desperate to learn more. My stomach rumbled as if I hadn't eaten in days, but I'd just stuffed myself like a pig. It was really only beginning to hit me. Strange as it may have seemed, I felt closer to Luz. I hoped in my silly and infantile view of romance that this could bring us even closer together and make right what wasn't possible for my mother and Luz's dad.

"You must have loved him a lot," Mom said.

"My papa was a good man."

"It's so strange I sometimes talk about him as if he's part of the family and I'm just waiting for him to drop by."

"I need to come clean," Luz said.

"What is it?" Mom said.

"I feel like I'm always explaining myself," Luz said. "And it never comes out right. I've been tracking you down. It took me a while to come to the States. It's not the sole reason I came here. I left Mexico because I needed a new beginning. It was too cozy there. I love my family, but they're happy with a big traditional, can't get two seconds to think by yourself family. That's just not me."

"How long have you been looking for me?"

"It took me a few times to even find the courage to ring your bell. The time I did I just ran off. I wasn't ready. I was still wrestling feelings of guilt and hate. My mother must have known; how could she not have? I was sorry she suffered, but we never spoke of it. How did you meet him?"

"He was a tour guide," Mom said. "I was sketching a woman on the street selling sweetbread. I wasn't even a part of his tour. He made the whole bus stop and watch me sketching. I hated having all those people breathing over my shoulders. He asked me to join his tour, but I told him no."

"So then what happened?"

"I joined the tour the next day, but when I did there was this bosomy woman from Texas who kept fawning over him. I was jealous, but I wasn't going to play her game. Turned out he couldn't stand her, she wore too much cheap cologne and when we stopped for a bite to eat he promised to show me the city at night. I told him I had to think about it."

"But you went along with him?" Luz said.

"Of course. I didn't find out he was married until my last visit. The same day the soccer team, America won the championship. The streets along Reforma were swimming in blue and gold jerseys."

"America's colors."

"What a weird name for a Mexican team. I pretended I was confused by it. The whole city chanting with pride, it was amazing. We were both so happy. I didn't want it to end and I insisted on eloping but he kept laughing saying that we should tell his wife first. He had that kind of personality and I told him to stop joking. I can't believe I didn't realize until then. When he stayed quiet I knew he wasn't kidding anymore."

"You really didn't know?" Luz asked.

"Maybe I was in denial. When you love somebody your brain becomes your arch enemy. You pump foolish hope where only reason belongs."

"I don't really know you, but I believe you. Part of me never wanted to meet you, but the other part had to."

"He must have been a great father."

"He might have been a better father than a husband, but my mother loved him. I made papa tell me he loved me more than my mother. He egged me on. I clipped his toenails, fixed his favorite meal, pozolé. It tasted awful because I didn't know how to make it, but he ate it anyway."

"I fought with my sisters for my father's affection," Mom said. "I shined his shoes, mended his pants. He died when I was your age, but I don't think I could've taken it if I was a teenager."

"You must have loved him a lot," Luz said.

"It's so strange I sometimes talk about my father as if he'll walk through the door at any moment."

Aunt Chloe nosed into the kitchen at that moment. When she couldn't take Mom and Luz staring at her any longer she fetched herself a chocolate turkey and gobbled its head.

"They're getting antsy out there," Aunt Chloe said.

"Tell them to keep their pants on," Mom said.

Aunt Chloe headed for the bathroom. That's when I hit the panic button. I'd been an expert eavesdropper for years, but when Aunt Chloe pulled the door open and revealed my whereabouts I felt I crossed the line. I stood like a dunce, an actor who lost his lines and didn't want to improvise or pick up on the part that I knew. My mouth felt dry and my eyes were itchy. I lurched forward so as not to seem scared, but trembled. My socks grew damp inside my snug-fitting shoes.

After this awkward discovery, both Mom and Luz arched their brows as I passed them. Mom let the plates slide into the bubbling sink. Then the three of us went over to the table and collected the pies, coffee and sugar cookies. Some discombobulated wait staff we made taking the goodies into the living room. The guests traded bobbled-headed nods and lent stilted, quivering chuckles. Home sweet homebodies. They all wanted to be anywhere else and I wanted to plumb deeper into the heart of Mom's past.

It took a while for everybody to leave. Aunt Chloe was the last to go, two plastic bags of goodies wedged under both arms. Thanksgiving may have been the one holiday guests left with more than they came with, proportionately speaking. Christmas usually holds a gift for gift trading quota, though loosely enforced. At our Thanksgivings, guests made out like bandits.

Luz stayed. Dad heated a fresh pot of coffee and Mom put out a spread of fruit, cheese and crackers. All too civilized if you asked me. Maybe Mom wanted Luz to see the family's better-bred, softer side. Mom sat with a photo album open on her lap. She walked Luz through nursery school, trick-or-treating and Little League shots.

"Benny loved dressing up and posing for pictures," Mom said.

"Why's he wearing a ski mask?" Luz asked.

"He was doing his Star Wars Cantina scene," Mom said. "Which one were you there, Snaggletooth?"

"Walrus Man," I said. "And Teddy and Congo were standing in for Han Solo and Chewbacca."

"He always made good use of his stuffed animals," Mom said.

"What a cute boy?" Luz said kissing my head.

"Are we going to keep boring her to tears?" I said.

Dad entered with the fresh pot of coffee. Mom got up and refilled her glass with Champagne. She grabbed the glass like a mug of beer and took a healthy swig.

"How about a fresh pour?" Mom said.

She didn't wait for Luz to give the go ahead, but filled the plastic party cup. Luz scooched toward the edge of the sofa and without putting either elbow on the table she managed to dip herself low enough to bring her mouth to the lip of the cup. She sipped an inch off the top. Bubbles rushed to the bottom of the plastic stem in a wicked, undulating spiral. I thought of a double helix.

"Let me see some of those," Dad said placing his coffee mug on the table. He adjusted the screw connecting the wire frame to his glasses before putting them on. He pointed to a photo. Mom parried his move keeping his finger off the page.

"That's Shelter Island," Dad said. "Look at all that seaweed. Looks like the creature from the Blue Lagoon all shriveled up."

Luz slapped her side to curb her rippling laugh.

"You always make the same mistake. It's Fire Island, Fair Harbor," Mom corrected.

"Are you sure?"

"Would you please tell him?" Mom said to the sofa-bound jury. "Benny was too small to swim when we went to Shelter Island."

"I don't know about that," Dad said. He angled the photo into the light. "Lucy, would you like some crackers?"

"Her name is Luz," Mom and I both chimed.

"You can call me Lucy, Mr. Fluke. Nobody's called me that before, but it sounds nice the way you say it."

"Mr. Fluke's got a short memory. He'll call you Luanna before the night's over."

"That's okay," Luz said.

"You're so agreeable," Mom said.

"Let's not go off on a tangent," I said. "I hate to put an end to your little party, but I'd like to clear a few things up."

"Like what?" Mom said.

"Well, does he know?" I said pointing at Dad.

"Listen Benny, we had a life before you were born. Both of us," Mom said.

"But you don't have to flaunt it," I said.

"Hey, have a little respect for your mother," Dad said.

"And does she respect you?"

"We have plenty of respect for each other."

"So we just pour this out in front of a stranger?" I said.

"Luz isn't a stranger," Mom said. "Why would you bring her over to a family gathering? You've never done that before."

"I know."

"So you must love her."

Luz sat closer to me. The warmth of her leg gave me an electric shock. Primal attraction coursed through my veins. A molten rock fist lumped in my belly. It still was difficult picturing Luz in the same room with my parents. I didn't worry about them judging her and it shocked me that I wasn't concerned about her judging them. What I had trouble with was the fact that Mom and Dad now saw Luz and knew that I wanted her, and more than that I was, however baby-stepped, easing her into the family. She bowled right in though, nothing easy about her welcoming. Under less complicated circumstances it would have been tough, but given the circumstances her place almost seemed arranged and waiting for her. A full-fledged initiation.

I considered Mom's point that I'd never asked anybody over, not to any family gatherings. I'd never thought so seriously about anybody. Luz was a whole different ballgame. I was happy she demanded coming over, though the shake-up was a bit hard to swallow. The good part was we were connected. What troubled me though was if she had satisfied what she had set out to do and there was nothing left.

While the album went around, I picked up one of the envelopes. The postage date was after I was born.

"How many times did you go to Mexico?" I asked.

"Three times," Mom said.

"So you took me along or did you stick with a babysitter?"

"I never went back after you were born."

"Hmm."

"What's hmm for?" Mom said.

"Read the date on the letter."

"I don't have to."

"Would you mind explaining why it's dated after I was born?"

"Tell him Ben Senior, tell your son," Mom said.

"You tell him," Dad said.

Mom reached for her glass and finished her bubbly.

"Your father was at a crossroads. He was a bit of a religious nut even then. He wanted to be a priest."

"No way?"

"It's true," Mom said.

"I don't believe it."

"It is true Benny," Dad said. "I had a calling. At least I thought I did. I was trying to figure things out. Your mother and I really didn't know each other so well. She wanted to go her own way."

"I told your father to pick me or the church," Mom interjected.

"Is that so?"

"Your mother didn't give me the chance to think things through. And we ended on a pretty harsh note. We didn't speak for a month and then she called me one night and told me she was pregnant."

"And you were pissed," I said. "But you did the honorable thing and married her."

"It wasn't like that at all. When your mother told me she was pregnant, for the first time in a long while, I had this crystal clear view. Everything seemed ripe. Colors grew bold. I knew then that I wanted to be a father."

"Don't give me that, you waited forever. Neither of you were young."

"Well, that's true. I wasn't so happy before that. Maybe I'd turned to the church for some answers, for some guidance. You should do that every so often it wouldn't kill you," Dad said.

"Benny, you can't blame me, your father had his past too," Mom said.

"I don't want to hear it."

"We both love you, don't you know that."

I watched Luz's expression sprawl with curious delight. Her boundless radiance and cherubic brown eyes made me shy when she fixed on me. Her portraiture belonged in the Uffizi, The Metropolitan. I wondered what was going through her mind, if she saw herself fitting into this family. I pinched my forefinger to my thumb as if trying to squish all the insecurities that ever rushed through me. A fat tear slid down my cheek.

When you realize that your mother loved somebody besides your father, reality sinks in that you, in this case I, might never have been born. What if she never met my dad?

Mom, as she often tells the story, had read a fortune after a General Tsao's chicken and egg drop soup lunch that she would meet her special someone during a near death experience. In fact, my father rescued her from the delivery boy racing on his bicycle. The kid didn't see her when he peeled into the intersection and my father, who happened to be the kind of person who was always looking out to make sure children and mothers with strollers crossed the street to safety, saw a woman in danger. He pulled her from harm's way.

You'd think the two were well on their way to living happily ever after, but what really brought them together was the ensuing argument because my father had ripped my mother's blouse. She yelled at him right there on the corner and when some random woman stopped to ask if my mother was alright and my mother told her what happened, the woman belted my father with her purse, thinking he was some kind of pervert.

Months later, after my father had a chance to explain what really had happened, Mom had a change of heart. She was rather taken by his charm and handsome smile.

He may not have been the true love of her life and I might never truly know whose spot that was reserved for – Juan Carlos, my father or some other dude lurking out there – but I was going to have to come to terms with it.

Luz had lunch with my mother, just the two of them to sort things out, perhaps to finally accept what was real, since the turn of events during Thanksgiving was so surreal. They could really talk with each other without the pests of Aunt Belinda or my father and of course without me snooping on them. No matter how impartial I claimed to be this was something I was still coping with.

I'd spent too many years neuter, a body without a pulse and then poof in no time I'd fallen for Luz, pumping breath and blood into my system. The turn of events, as strange as it may have seemed, in some warped way increased my odds of winning over Luz. I was almost hopeful that she'd found her father's spirit alive and well in me, in my family, and that by staying with me she'd find part of herself that she'd thought was gone forever.

The whole while they were opening themselves up to each other I was taking stock of all that had happened in such a short span. My life is best summed up as Punctuated Equilibrium, a theory purported by the late Stephen Jay Gould. It basically suggests that for large chunks of time the earth remains static, in other words without much geological fanfare. Then after these long chunks of stability some monumental changes unfurl. Cataclysmic events, mass extinctions, that sort of thing wipe out flora, fauna and animals and those few brave souls who make it through carry their lineage into a new direction.

Luz was my catalyst, my catapult. She launched me further then I believed I could go. Maybe I rose to the occasion to impress her. Who knows?

"You've punctuated my equilibrium," I told her, shoving the new television through our doorway.

"I didn't mean to," she said, scrutinizing my arm for the mark she thought she'd made.

It went much deeper. She cut right into my essence, with razor sharpness. She knew me, saw things within me, as if my soul floated beside me, inert, naked. She touched my delicate side. Of course I was angry with her because I thought she'd used me to understand a part of her self that she thought was missing. I didn't want to come off as being too forgiving, too much of a pushover, but maybe I used her. Maybe I needed a boost to get going with my life. How long was I planning on living with those nuts, my parents? Luz got me to move out on my own. She shaped things for me that I played off as silly whims. She nudged me into my book business. She saw me doing things I was too afraid to put into words, she saw them in me, without the aid of brain scanners and giant screens. Maybe her vision came from within herself. Introspection can solve great problems in somebody else. In any event, she read me and when she shared her wisdom she didn't sugarcoat anything, saying crap like you'll be a great writer someday.

She tacked a memo about Abraham Lincoln onto our refrigerator and it took me a few days before I actually read it. It listed his failures. Of course, I assumed she was trying to say something more about us, maybe use some reverse psychology, because of the way things turned out. I didn't want to think that it was going to be over just yet. I still hadn't mentioned anything about going off to France, but I was going to keep that in my back pocket in case she decided to cut out on me again.

I picked up the list of Lincoln failures. He lost just about every political race you could think of, multiple times. He came from humble beginnings, no trust funds, cattle ranches or legacies to squeeze him into office. He was, to put it mildly, a poster boy for failure and look how he turned out.

"Whacked in a theatre house," I said.

"That's not it and you know it," Luz said. "He became who he was because of torment, never able to reconcile or accept defeat."

"So what am I supposed to do, become president?"

"You're supposed to look inside yourself and become something you've been too cowardly to admit to wanting. Do that and you'll move mountains. At the very least, you'll sleep better."

"Why should I care how I sleep? Look, I'm not going for these bogus dreams of fame and fortune. I won't be a cube rat for umpteen years so I can run this one horse town."

"Sometimes I think you're so smart, even when you blather on with all this philosophical nonsense that frankly, nobody really cares about. Sometimes you're so passionate. How do you lose that?"

"I don't know. I just don't see the point sometimes."

"Nobody does, but when the fog dies down and you can see again you begin to realize this isn't some dress rehearsal. This is our life. Good, bad or blah. Make an utter fool of yourself. You know you're not afraid to. I've seen you dance."

***

Sleep's a chore. When I do conk out sketches from childhood invade me. I'm stuck in this drab trapezoidal room, without windows or doors. The dimensions seem crooked, the floorboards warped, sterile, with a faint whiff of mothballs and Windex. Everybody sports uniforms. The girls in pleated skirts, white shirts and green boleros, the boys in blue corduroys, white shirts with green ties, and I'm noodling with mine, trying to make a Windsor knot but it turns out to be a clip-on and across from me Thelonious sits atop a garbage can, rattling it with a spoon. With his free hand, he points his knobby finger laughing at me.

The boys, chewing on crayons, draw pictures of my mother in her bikini doing handstands while the girls sketch Juan Carlos as a reclining nude, the stupid boys, monkeys included, keep snickering at the girls' work, and, to tell you the truth, they were doing a good job. Their shading enhances his musculature.

It took a while for me to slice out of the dream but when I did I recalled some strange sketching classes that I'd attended with my mother as a child. She worked on nudes, well-proportioned, long-haired men on dirt roads, skinning fruit, while others sluiced through water. Juan Carlos was always Mom's muse, his lingering spirit now layered with flesh and bone.

Footnote

She let me walk with her and the dogs: Gene Simmons, the Akita, and a fluffy pug new to the clan. Luz waggled the rest of the leashes.

"I'm going to throw this out to you," I said. "What if we go to France together?"

"For how long?" Luz said.

"I've always wanted to pick grapes."

"But that's so far off."

"We don't have to wait till harvest. How about grabbing cheap seats and find an off-the-beaten-path estate and prune vines?"

"Are you serious?"

"I just want us to be together."

"And here we are."

We sized each other up for the moment. Neither wanted to admit it, but it was so obvious on her face. I felt a crinkle by my mouth, the bane of blushing ready to sell me out. The crisp autumn breeze nipped my ears while the blood orange sun still blared off my cheeks making my momentary homeostasis all the more flummoxing.

"Look Benny, don't get upset, but I'm going to make you finish your thesis."

"No way. Come on."

"I'm not kidding. You can't let it slide.

"I'm not."

"Then when are you going to wrap it up?"

Just then I felt the dogs pulling me in a million directions. But I was only leashing three of them. My thoughts crossed lanes. I could almost feel myself peeking into my brain again. A bright, muzzy, phosphorescent stream of colors, sounds, and smells collided. It was synesthetic, transcendental.

I couldn't digest. I wished to touch the skin of the sublime. Nothing connected. Precious onyx notes wafted from Luz's soft wet lips. Then a rollicking jolt ran up my ankles. It squeezed between my ears. All I wanted was for our bond to set an indestructible suture. I warbled something and she slapped my arm. My ears rung and my tongue scratched dry as sandpaper.

Sweat slivered down my back. I almost read the words off her lips. I crushed the leash and eyed the dogs. They startled me, but I bit my tongue.

"You better be there to help me," Luz said.

"Of course I can," I said, probably too loud as if I just cracked a homer.

"Good. Because somebody needs to hold the camera while I question our trusty Luddites."

"I'm your man."

"The first interview is set."

"With who?'

"Your buddy Brig."

"Yeah, I guess he's techno-challenged."

"Uh-huh."

We let go of the dogs once we entered the pen. They dashed off like greyhounds chasing the interstices between nature and nurture.

"Hey Luz, are you ever going to tell me about you and Brig?"

"Let's make a pact."

"How so?"

"No more prying into the past. And if all goes well, we'll pick grapes together next harvest."

"Anywhere I want?"

"First, you finish your thesis."

We basked in the late a.m. sun, leaves aflutter and the ground tilted again.

"Feel like going to the zoo?" Luz said.

"What about the mutts?"

"We drop them off, then it's my treat."

"On one condition."

"Name it."

"We set loose the monkeys."

"I'm game if you are."

About the Author

John Gorman's stories have been published in Mississippi Review, The Shore, Nexus, Quarterly Literary Review of Singapore, The Rose and Thorn, Word Riot, Monkeybicycle, and elsewhere. He won the 2003 NY Int'l Indie Film and Video Festival screenplay competition with For the Love of Auntie. He lives in New York City.

ALL THINGS THAT MATTER PRESS ™

FOR MORE INFORMATION ON TITLES AVAILABLE FROM
ALL THINGS THAT MATTER PRESS, GO TO
http://allthingsthatmatterpress.com
or contact us at
allthingsthatmatterpress@gmail.com

www.ingramcontent.com/pod-product-compliance
Lightning Source LLC
Chambersburg PA
CBHW031111260626
47172CB00001B/322